To

Miss Kelly
Hope you
Enjoy the
Book

IT'S GONNA RAIN

A NOVEL BY

JEFFERY ROSHELL

Also By Jeffery Roshell

ThornHill High School

RoWash Publishing Presents:

IT'S GONNA RAIN

Author: Jeffery Roshell

ISBN-13: 978-1534897816

ISBN-10: 153489781X

LCCN: TBD

Editing/Typesetting: Young Dreams Publications – Ty Waller
www.youngdreamsbig.com

Connect with Jeffery Roshell

jefferyroshell@facebook.com

www.jefferyroshell.net

IG: authorjefferyroshell

Acknowledgements

As always, I want to start out by THANKING GOD, without him none of this would be possible. Justin Q. Young another cover well done, bro! My high school classmate and sister, Ty Waller, thank you so much for helping with this project! My publishing company, Rowash Publishing, lets continue to put out good reads for the readers.

My brothers for life, Eye'Am Malone and Mark Taylor, when you two could have said no, you said yes instead and for that I am forever grateful! My family, friends, co-workers, new author friends, and reading fans, let me just say that I am beyond excited to be a part of the literary world, showing off my own talent. Dr. John Mostrando, Author BlackWidow, Lashone O'Connor, Vondra Donette Flowers (R.I.P.), Fredrick Reed, Sharnel Williams, April Freeman, The Cortiva Institute, Tammy Jernigan, Michele Dawn Mellette, Kenya Ervin & Soul Sistah's Book Club, Rebekah Cole, Janice Elmore & The South Holland Public Library, Veronica Bell, Marilyn Bell, Kisha Green, Radiah Hubbert, Michelle Davis, and also to you, who took the time to purchase this next installment by me! Enjoy.

Dedicated to the late great, E. Lynn Harris.

CHAPTER ONE

MARILYN

I grabbed my purse, iPhone, garment bag - which had my choir robe in it - and my Bible. It was thirty-five degrees outside on a Sunday morning in March in Chicago. I took one last look at myself in my living room mirror glancing over my long, red pea coat, the red heels that I had on matching the red skirt and white top underneath it. I put on my church hat letting my long jet black hair flow down my back. I opened the front door stepping out of my two-story, three-bedroom home. I was glad the snow was holding off – I was hoping it was done since the last snow fall we had was back

in January. I'd take the cold weather over the snow any day
- especially if I didn't drive in the snow to work every day.
Chicago weather was funny like that. It could go from brisk
cold to pleasantly warm within a matter of seconds.

"Good morning, Marilyn!" I heard my next door
neighbor, Estelle, say as I turned my head in her direction.
She was a sixty-year-old white widow who I loved to pieces.
Estelle was so bubbly and opened her arms to me and my
family when we first moved into The Beverly neighborhood
fifteen years ago.

"Hey, Estelle!" I said smiling at her.

"I'm on my way to mass." She said walking to her car.

"Yes, we gotta give him the praise not just on Sunday
but everyday!" I said.

"He's the author and finisher of our faith." Estelle
responded as she was opening the door to her black, 2014
Buick Lasabre she'd just purchased last year. She was a
retired high school English teacher, and her husband had
retired from the railroad before he passed about three years
ago. She had a daughter and a son who were thirty-seven
and thirty-nine years old; they would visit her every now and
then, usually just checking on their mother to make sure she
was okay. Estelle waved before speeding off. She attended
one of the Catholic churches in the downtown area of

Chicago, but I could not think of the name or the location because it was so many.

Coming around the corner from the garage was my black, 2013 Dodge Charger with my oldest son, Marquise, driving it. He had his own black, 2012 Toyota Camry, but on Sundays we usually rode to church together. Marquise had to be in the pulpit sitting with the other associate pastors, the same time I had to be in the choir stand. I always sat on the first row in the soprano section, I was always on time, and I had a thing about being late. I won't say I haven't been late in the past, but for the most part, I made sure that nothing stopped me from getting to the house of God on time. I walked down the front steps, got into the car, buckled my seatbelt as I was closing the door, and Marquise began speeding down Western Avenue.

"Did you move them boxes in the garage?" I asked him.

"Yes." He said smiling shaking his head, but concentrating on the road.

"Good because I need you and Tice to clean everything out of there when the weather breaks." I said looking at him as he made a face.

I loved my oldest and was proud of the man he was becoming. He was the youth pastor at our church, he had a full-time job, and he was a full-time college student at Chicago State studying Information Technology. And don't let me leave out the fact that he could sing; which is something that he inherited from me. Not just harmonizing, he could really sing the roof off of any place. Even though he was not in the church choir, the director would ask him to lead certain songs every now and then, the congregation and pulpit would be moved by his voice each and every time he got up to sing. For twenty-four years old, I was, indeed, happy that he had accomplished so much and was still getting better each and every day.

Then there was my other son Martice - the baby boy. You would think that the youngest would be the one that you would have the least amount of problems with, and expect the oldest to give you the most hell - but it was the other way around. Martice was so much like his daddy, slick, sneaky, and loved to talk back. When I married Rick Johnson he was forty and I had just turned twenty. My mother was not happy about it and begged me to reconsider. But try telling that to a nose-opened young woman in love with a handsome man twice her age; old enough to almost be her daddy. I fell in love with Rick because he was extremely attractive, and he looked no older than thirty when we first met. He had a muscular frame; he was six-foot-three, light-skinned with a high top fade, and a deep voice that could grab the attention of any woman that he wanted. Well it certainly caught my

4

attention – had me so mesmerized that I ignored that he had two failed marriages prior to me due to cheating and gambling and that he was about to make me wife number three, repeating the same pattern. His first wife, Betty, whom he had three daughters with, tried to warn me - but instead of listening I thought that she was just jealous and wanted him back. I wasn't too off in my assumption; I could have been her little sister because of the age difference, I think I would have been jealous, too. But how I wish like hell I would have listened to what she was saying.

I was in the Jewel-Osco grocery store the day she spotted me. She had her three girls tugging along with her; at that time their oldest was twelve, the middle child was ten, and the baby girl was five. She pulled me to the side and muttered these words, "Good luck and be careful!" I'd never forget how she grinned and walked off with their three girls looking back at me. Those words haunted my life for the next fifteen years before he passed in 2005 from prostate cancer.

Being the third wife, I had gained all of the same drama that he put his previous wives through and then some because I had to deal with the ex-wife drama; but inherited all of his money, and I'd say that was a fair compensation. Rick had a pension from when he retired from the railroad, and also had ten-thousand dollars his grandfather left for him in a savings account. He never touched that money in the saving account, but left it to me for when Martice reached twenty-one. I've yet to tell him about it because I know he would go out of his mind and act a fool with that amount of money.

Rick left his three daughters each a fair share amount, but Betty didn't feel that it was a fair share – she'd expected for her daughters to get far more than what Rick left for them. To me, the money was split the way it should have been; her kids got their share, me and mine did as well. For the last seventeen years I've worked as the billing department supervisor for Blue Cross and Blue Shield Health Insurance. Retirement would be coming very early and soon within the next few years and I was definitely looking forward to it.

"Why the face?" I asked Marquise. But I didn't give him a chance to respond because I faintly heard my jam, "Amazing" by Ricky Dillard & New Generation Chorale in the background. I slightly turned the volume dial up – I loved this song it was slow and very heartfelt.

Marquise turned the music back down some to respond to my question. "Cause you always got somethin' for me and Tice to do, Mama. As if we have nothin' to do on that day or sumthin'." He said shaking his head.

I turned slightly and looked at him. "Well excuse me for needing my garage cleaned out of what most of the stuff in there belongs to you, anyway." I said sarcastically while giving him the Black-woman head shake.

He grinned a little. "Yea, you're right mama..." He said shaking his head.

My Response was "Uh-huh", as we stopped at Bishop Barron C. Winston Drive and he put on the left hand signal to turn. Marquise drove into the main parking lot of the church and parked in the back.

"We can discuss this later." I said to him as I was gathering my garment bag, Bible, iPhone, and purse while getting out of the car and closing the door. He looked at me and smiled again. My son had a way of just giving a facial expression that would speak for his actual words. Walking, we both got to the old sanctuary and decided to take the short cut like we always did each Sunday - going through the doors into the newer sanctuary. It was a good thing that Bishop Winston did not do what most pastors would have by tearing the old sanctuary down, or turning it into something else, or even selling it to another pastor whose congregation outgrew a much smaller building that they had. Instead he kept it, and would sometimes let the choirs use it for rehearsals, if need be.

Everything was still the way we left it in the old sanctuary from the day we marched from the old building to the new. The old church was our main sanctuary from 1970 until the summer of 2000. We've now been in the new building the past fifteen years. The majority of Powerhouse's major events and choir musicals happened in the old sanctuary over the years, which was all a part of the churches history. I can remember a line wrapped around the door starting at around 10 am every Sunday morning. Once the eight-hundred seated building was filled to capacity, the ushers had no choice but to turn others away that were still coming. Powerhouse was known for Bishop Winston's power preaching and The Voices of Powerhouse.

The Voices of Powerhouse was the church's choir, whom I have sung with in the soprano section for the last twenty-three years. We had just finished our third live recording three months ago. The radio stations from Chicago and across the world were anticipating it so they could play some of the songs, or at least one that was a hit on the radio before the CD released in July of this year. The Voices of Powerhouse were organized by Samuel Watson and his wife Mabel in 1970, when the church first started. Mabel was our organist until she passed in 1998 due to a brain aneurysm. The choir went from thirty members in the beginning days, to a total of one hundred members today. There was never an empty seat at the choir musicals, or even our radio broadcast that used to come on in the middle 70's; until they stopped in the late 80's. At that time we started coming on television every Sunday night at 8pm.

As I got closer to the new main sanctuary, I saw some of the choir members and members of the congregation. They greeted me with normal Sunday morning hellos, hugs, and the side kisses on the cheek, those especially came from the mothers of the church. I walked through the glass doors of the beautiful main sanctuary which had purple cushioned pews and purple carpet on the floor, the floor seated about seven thousand people, and the balcony seated about a thousand. The choir stand chairs were purple, the wall behind the choir stand had a huge gold cross on it in the middle,

with the inscription under it going across in big bold purple letters: "THERE IS POWER IN THE CROSS".

I made it to the choir room which was in the back of the pulpit and choir stand, where I was greeted by more choir members. I took off my coat and hung it up, while placing my hat on the top shelf. I put my purse, cell phone, and Bible on the table because they were going to the choir stand with me. I unzipped my garment bag with my robe inside which was all white with a gold overlay, putting the robe on first, then putting the overlay on next to go over the robe.

"Marilyn, let me zip you up." Sharon Riley, my soprano section sister said. I turned my back toward her and she zipped up the robe mid-way to give my neck and throat a little room to still breathe.

"Thanks!" I said to her smiling patting my hair a little as I picked up her compact mirror to make sure my make-up and hair was still in place. She had laid it on the table after fixing her own hair and make-up.

"Marilyn you must be so proud of Marquise, now? With him becoming youth pastor of the church and add to that he's dating Bishop's granddaughter!" She said putting on her robe.

I turned in her direction, smiled, and said, "Yes, I am!"

Thinking back, Bishop Winston has always treated Marquise like he was his own son since he was a little boy. I can always remember Bishop, on any given Sunday, calling on Marquise to either read a scripture or sing a song. Bishop would yell in the mic, "This is my spiritual son, but I treat him like he's one of my own."

"Girl, I hope he has plans on becoming the pastor once Bishop steps down. Marquise really preaches some good sermons on youth Sundays. My kids love to hear him when he preaches and sings." Daphne, one of the altos, said. I heard quite a few others from the choir that were now in the room with us agreeing.

"And how is Martice?" She asked.

I looked at her and nonchalantly said, "He's doing okay."

I noticed that the choir members were heading out the door towards the choir stand. It was time for praise and worship before service started. I grabbed my purse, putting the strap on my shoulder, then my Bible, and iPhone. I started walking toward the sanctuary to take my place on the first row in the soprano section of the choir stand, that's when I heard Daphne ask walking right behind me. "And who's Martice dating with his handsome self?"

CHAPTER TWO

MARTICE

I heard my Galaxy S5 cell phone ring next to my bed on my table. I reached over, tapped the speakerphone button without looking at the screen or phone - that's just how skilled I was with my phone. "Yea…" I said as I answered in a groggy voice.

"Martice? Martice? Bitch, wake up." The caller said to my greeting.

"Chile, what you want at 10:45 in the am on a Sunday?" I said to my best friend, Treyshawn.

"To talk about last night. Girlllllllllll, that party was off the chain wasn't it?" He said sounding like he was still on cloud nine from last night.

"It was alright. It wasn't nothin' to go home to mama about." I said sitting up and pushing the covers away from my body. I had on a black tank top and my Chicago Bears' pajama pants with no socks. I rubbed the sleep out of my eyes, grabbed my remote and hit the on button to my TV. *I should have went to church this morning.* I said to myself knowing that my mother was going to have something to say when her and my brother came in from service.

"Did you see that dude that was all up in your face last night at the club?" Treyshawn said.

"Yeah, and I wasn't goin'. You know damn well I'm not tryin to give nothin' that don't look like they, remotely, have a job, car, or money in their pocket the time of day. You could tell he was a bum ass nigga." I said flipping the channels with the remote, shaking my head as I pictured last night again. This dude was trying to get my number, telling me how he had this and that and all types of bank accounts, but had on a pair of thirty dollar Converse and an outfit that I know I seen at Forman Mills - *The Cheap Store* from the men's section. I went in there last week with Treyshawn because his ass shopped there. I was all about Macy's,

13

DTLR, Express for Men, ALDO, and Footlocker just ask my closet; it spoke for itself.

"Well the sissies love to make themselves appear to be more than what they are not." Treyshawn said.

"That's all the time! Which is why I an't goin'! I told his thirty-five year old ass to move around, miss me with the lies or go find you another one in here to sell that story too." I said with sass in my voice.

"Chile, you know you be letting them have it." Treyshawn said laughing.

"I don't be tryin' to but they bring it out of me." I said getting up and putting my Bluetooth LG Headset around my neck and in my ears so that I could go downstairs and fix myself something to eat for breakfast.

"Chile, your mama and brother gone to Sunday service, honey?" Treyshawn asked trying to be funny.

"Yep, I heard them when they left. I'm shocked my mother wasn't beatin' on my door askin' me why I was not up getting ready for church this morning." I said.

"Chile, you still think your mother and brother don't know you a sissy, honey?"

I had to give the phone the once over look. I don't know how many times I cringed at that question, especially when Treyshawn would ask me. "No they don't. So stop

14

asking me." I said irritated like any other time he would bring this up. The phone was silent and then he burst out laughing,

"Girl, yo mama and yo brother know about you they just waitin' on your ass to come out the closet... especially yo mama. Mama's always know." Treyshawn said matter-of-factly.

"Well mine don't." I sharply added.

"Naw, honey. You think Miss Marilyn don't know but she do." Treyshawn concluded.

I sighed and said. "Next subject!"

"I guess. I forgot you get all sensitive when I talk about that. So I'm not gonna even mention it no more." He said sarcastically.

"Good, cause I'm tired of talking about it!" I said with a little attitude.

My thing was just because Treyshawn's family knew about him, because he was all out and feminine as hell, that had nothing to do with my mother or brother. It wasn't so much that I did not identify with being gay, but growing up I heard so much wrong about it. The world frowns down on gays; this is why I suppressed my feelings and hid them from my family. I battled so many emotional demons throughout the last years since I have been in the lifestyle. My mother

15

was so proud of my brother Marquise and the many accomplishments that he has achieved. My mother rarely ever praised me on anything, which at times hurts but I have just dealt with it in spite of. However, I think the rejection has made me become the rebel out of us two. I was the one that got into trouble, did not give a shit about anything, I really possessed a "fuck you, it's about me" attitude.

I heard a buzz in my ear and saw my phone screen light up from the table. I knew it was some dude from *Jack'd* - a gay hook-up app which showed you guys that were close or near your area. Within the app you could respond via messaging to a private message sent from one user to the next. I went over to the phone and checked the message. " SUP!" was all it said and I proceeded to scrolled the unknown user's profile. All pictures were private and not showing.

"Open your pics." I typed and hit send.

"What's goin on for today? Treyshawn asked.

"Nothin'. I'll probably hit the gym and come back and just watch Real House Wives." I said glancing at my phone letting me know I had a message from whomever this was hitting me up on *Jack'd*. I hit the message button and his pictures were opened – and he was fine as hell! I immediately responded to him. "Where are you? Mobile? Or are you hosting?"

16

"Yea, I'm waitin' on Miss Housewives, honey! You know I love me some NeNe, Bitch!" Treyshawn said with such flamboyant sassiness.

"Chile...." I said laughing, but somewhat distracted as I'm waiting on the anonymous user's response.

My phone buzzed, the message read, "Off Keening and Western."

I was intrigued because that was about ten minutes from my house. I typed, "What you tryin' to get into?" Then I hit send.

"You know Miss NeNe and Kandi keeps it real! Plus NeNe makes the show honey; wouldn't be right without her." Treyshawn said.

I had to agree with him, NeNe did make the show. She was one of the reasons that I watched and continued as another season would start one after another. I got the response back from my *Jack'd* pursuer five minutes later and it was a damn paragraph about what he wanted to do, which raised my eyebrow and got me hot. He also stated he was mobile looking to come out. Now normally I didn't invite anyone to my house for a hookup because there are so many nuts and weirdos, but from the stats in his profile compared to my five-foot-ten, one hundred and ninety-eight pound, all muscular frame I wasn't worried about nothing

17

popping off with him when he got over here. I typed my cell phone number and told him to text me so I could text him my address.

"Well next weekend is Jamar's party." Treyshawn said.

Jamar was friends with Treyshawn. I'd met him almost two years ago. Jamar was very grand (meaning he thought he was the shit). Jamar had attended a private Catholic high school all of his four years. Attended North Carolina University his four years with a major in human resource management, and now he worked as an HR generalist for one of the highest paying companies in the state of Illinois. He never talked about how much his salary was but he would be quick to let someone know in a second not to try it cause he could "shit on them" as he would put it in a quick second, to me which was late (which meant not making any sense in gay terminology). I did not care for Jamar and his feelings were mutual toward me. He was very shady and always had a cut for any and everything. That's how it went in the gay life, some sissies you would be cool with, others you would say *bitch just die, and right now*.

"I don't know why you tellin' me about that bitch's party, I don't fuck with her." I said annoyed.

"Chile!" He said as I was shaking my head.

I became distracted from a new text message that was coming through my phone, I tapped my phone to read it. The message was the guy saying his name was Dee and that he would be my way in about fifteen minutes. My reply was "K". And was happy because this gave me enough time to jump in the shower and wash my ass before he came.

"Well, chile, hit me later." I said to Treyshawn.

"A'ight, honey, I will. And enjoy your *Jack'd* hook up." He said laughing.

"Fuck you, bitch." I said to him even though he was right which is why I laughed at the comment.

"Alright, talk to you later!" Treyshawn said laughing.

"Bye, bitch." I said clicking the line. I immediately went to get in the shower so that I could get ready. I knew my mother and bother would not be back home before my hookup got here. Which gave us plenty of time to hook up.

CHAPTER THREE

MARQUISE

I nodded my head and shouted a few Baptist "wells" as Bishop Winston preached about not worrying about the things you could not change in the world. I stood on my feet with the rest of the associate pastors in the pulpit as Bishop hollered and yelled bringing the message home. The choir started to stand up behind us.

"I said be not dismayed whatevaaaaaaaaaa be tides you... GOD, he will! He will! He will! He willllllll take care of you!!!!" Belted Bishop Winston.

The eight thousand plus members that packed out morning service were all on their feet, in the balcony and lower section of the sanctuary, yelling with Bishop Winston. Some waved their hands, and you heard a few "Amens!" and "Preach, Bishop". I glanced at the TV monitor on the left side on the wall, the camera was on the choir stand and my mother yelled out, "Say that bishop!" in her soprano voice.

I looked out into the congregation and met the smile of the other important lady in my life besides my mother, Bishop Winston's granddaughter, Isis. I smiled back. We started out as just friends for a long time since we both grew up in Powerhouse. Then it eventually grew to a mutual attraction. Our friends called us Ebony and Ivory because she was dark skinned and I was a light bright dude. Her pretty dark brown skin, just like my mothers, complemented her long, jet-black hair and her five-foot-seven, one hundred forty pound frame. Isis was one of the finest girls at the church, most of the young guys my age, or a little older that were single in the church were hating on me because Bishop gave me his definite blessing when he got word that we were dating. He said if anybody could court his granddaughter in the church he would want it to be me.

Bishop opened the doors of the church for people to join by candidate of baptism or letter of Christian experience. I heard the organ player start the tune of Reverend Milton Brunson and The Thompson Community Singers' popular gospel song, "Thank You". It was a very old church song and the only reason I knew it so well was because my mother led the solo part to it. Solomon handed her the mic as she stepped out of the choir stand, faced the congregation and started to sing; one thing's for sure I got my vocals from my mom; it also brought a thought to me about how she would always say that Martice inherited a lot of our father's ways. I missed my dad sometimes but GOD wanted him back sooner, and being a Christian I understood and made peace with that the last few years.

The congregation started to get up on their feet again and I heard a few screams of women catching the Holy Ghost. My mother started to walk down the steps of the pulpit. As one of the deacons helped her down, she started to sing to the congregation, people started walking one by one to the front to take seats in the chairs to join the church and give their life to the Lord. Isis and First Lady waved their hands at my mother as she continued to drive the song so effortlessly. My mother looked up at Solomon as he nodded for her to end and she brought the song home walking back up the steps and handing the mic to him, going back to the soprano section.

"Your brother gets on my last damn nerves because he could have brought his yellow ass to church." My mother said as we drove home after service. I shook my head because I knew this was coming just like every other Sunday

Martice did not go to church. "Then he comin' in the house all times of the night, hanging out with that strange boy that he calls a friend, Treyshawn. He need to get it together he will be twenty-two years old in two months." She nagged on while shaking her head.

"Ma, you're gonna get your blood pressure up." I said to her stopping at a red light.

"Well, thank GOD I still go workout at the gym and look good for forty-two." She replied back.

I laughed. "Oh, really!" I said pressing my foot on the gas when the light turned green.

"Yes! You know I look good as your mother for my age!" She said conceitedly.

Minister Davie Moore's "Dwell In Me" came on the radio and she turned up the volume. "I love this song!" She said bobbing her head as I did the same thing. We started singing along as we were getting closer and closer to the house. I pulled up and parked. We got out and my mother was hitting it up the steps in her heels; she was ready to lay into Martice's ass.

I know I shouldn't curse but I'm human; it wasn't like it was something I did a lot but every now and then I could still roll with the best of them. People expected so much of you once you got to a certain status when it came to being called into the ministry. Ministers still were human too and your faith should be in GOD not man anyway.

My mother opened the door laid her robe, purse, Bible, and phone on the table and yelled my brother's name. "MARTICE!!!" She yelled going into the kitchen as I walked in and locked the door behind me.

I sat down on the couch ready for the little show I was about to see before I went upstairs to get ready to go get something to eat with Isis. My brother came flying down the stairs. "Yeah?!" He said standing in the walkway of the living room which led to the kitchen.

"You can go out but can't come to church?" She asked him.

"My intent was to come but..." Martice said stuttering.

"But what?!" She snapped cutting him off. "You know what, don't even answer that." She said before he could respond to her. "You know the least you can do is go to church and give *GOD* some praise for what he continues to do for you. All you wanna do is run your ass up and down the damn streets with that boy. There was a time you used to come to church on a regular basis, matter of fact, you used to sing in the choir with me. So what happened?" She asked him with her hands on her hips.

"I..." He began to say.

"I nothing.." My mother said cutting him off again as I dropped my head and laughed. Martice had a smirk on his face as well because he knew he was pissing our mother off. She walked out to the living room to grab her garment bag with her robe in it, to hang it up in the closet. "Get back into church, Martice! People always askin' me about you." She said to him. My brother's expression changed and he started to look pissed off.

"Why are they asking about me?" He said with an attitude.

"Because they know I have two sons and not one. Therefore, you need to come back so that they know Marquise isn't the only boy I gave birth to." She said walking past him and into her bedroom which was right by the kitchen, the backdoor, and the door that led to the basement.

Martice shook his head and went back upstairs. I knew that whenever my mother would go there, that would piss him off. He did not like being compared to me. I got up and went upstairs to my room to change, shower, and let Isis know I would be at her house in thirty minutes to get her so we could go eat Sunday Dinner.

CHAPTER FOUR

MARILYN

Since Marquise and Bishops Granddaughter Isis were going out for dinner, which I did not know why when he could have just saved money and had Sunday dinner here at the house. I made spaghetti, garlic bread, a tossed salad, and a few pieces of baked chicken breast sprinkled with garlic seasoning and cut up red and green bell peppers on top for me and Martice.

Martice always liked the tossed salads I made because I put in green peppers, olives, parmesan cheese, feta cheese, onions, tomatoes, cucumbers, and shredded cheddar cheese. I loved the Hidden Valley brand ranch dressing, but the boys tended to like Thousand Island dressing better. My house phone rang as I was taking the baked chicken out of the oven to let it cool. I looked at the caller ID and it was my mother.

"Hello Mother!" I said putting the phone up to my ear and leaning my head to the side to hold it as I started tossing the salad with the salad tossers.

"Marilyn, how are you baby?" She asked me sounding like she was on her patio.

"Good, Mama!" I said.

"And how was church service today?" She asked.

"Great! Seven people joined church today." I said as I finished the salad, took out the garlic bread, and checked the spaghetti. In between I called out to Martice to come eat as I took two plates out of the glass cabinet along with two forks out of the drawer.

"Good. I miss Powerhouse so much I can't wait to come to Chicago in a few weeks." She said.

My mother would be here in time for Easter which was a good thing. My sister Marian would be happy to see our mother as well, but the truth be told she was closer to me than Marian.

"And how are the boys?" She asked.

28

"Marquise just went out with Bishop's granddaughter, Isis, for dinner. He's doin' great, working and goin' to school!" I said smiling.

"And Tice?" My mom asked.

I heard her ask me about Martice and a solemn look came on my face. I regretfully replied, "Martice is Martice."

"Marilyn, you don't sound so happy saying that." She said feeling my energy over the phone.

"Not at all mama. But Martice has changed a lot and I don't like it." I said as he walked into the kitchen and we locked eyes then he started fixing his plate.

"Marilyn, he's an adult. Shit, you probably getting on his last damn nerve. You know you were always the one with the controlling Cancer attitude. And Marian she's the complaining ass Capricorn." Hearing my mother talk about me and my sister, Marian, irritated me to the soul. She always did this when she thought I was in the wrong; calling me a controlling Cancer.

"And Mama what does that mean? That I'm controlling." I asked her. Martice had a smirk on his face; I gave him a look and adjusted the phone to my ear.

"You know Marquise has mentioned he's ready to move out. I asked him what your thoughts were..."

I sighed. "Mama, Marquise is not ready to move out, yet." I said.

"Marilyn, says who? You need to let the boy move out if he wants to. And I bet you ain't even told him or Martice about..."

I cut her off. "Mama, I will call you back I've been expecting this call that's coming through." I said fervently.

"Yeah." She said hanging up and I put the phone on the hook.

Martice gave me the "why you lying" look.

"Mind your business, okay?" I said to him getting up to fix my plate. "But while you are here, and it's just me and you, let's do some talking, mister!" I said to him as he rolled his eyes and started eating his spaghetti. "Martice, I love you. You are my baby boy but some of the things that you are doing I don't agree with."

"Like?" He said looking at me.

"Like the fact that you are running out with that Treyshawn boy every Saturday night. You hardly go to church anymore. And when are you going to start dating? There are a lot of nice girls at the church." I said to him breaking a piece of the garlic bread and eating it.

"Mama, I'm focused on working and getting myself back into school. All that other stuff can wait." He said.

I looked at him. Truth be told, my son was hiding something from me. Us mothers have that intuition, but if he was going to play the dummy role with me, I was going to play it back with him. I got up grabbed two cups and put ice in them.

"You want lemonade or juice?" I asked him.

"Ma, I could have gotten it myself." He said.

I looked at him poured myself some of the Country Time Lemonade and sat down. "Well pour it yourself. You saw me up and there was no reason why I couldn't have poured it for you." I said shaking my head.

He smacked his lips and got up to pour himself some cranberry juice. He also mumbled something under his breath.

"I didn't hear you." I said sternly with my eyebrows raised.

"Nothin.'" Was his response.

We sat in silence for five minutes before I broke it. "Martice I just want the relationship we had months ago; it's like you have changed and I don't know why."

He looked at me. "Ma, I haven't changed, but it just seems like nothing pleases you with me. All you do is praise Marquise. *Marquise this* and *Marquise that,* like he's your

31

only son. That's why we have no relationship like we use to." He said continuing to eat.

I was listening to him, but he was not about to tell me that I was the damn problem, oh, hell no. "Well what do you think I should do to be a better mother?" I said looking at him.

He looked up at me, dropped his fork, and shook his head, "You see, ma, it's that right there that just makes no sense at all." He said.

"What are you talkin' about!?" I snapped.

"You do that, ma. That thing right there. You're being sarcastic and I'm tellin you how I feel. You know, ma, I'm done eating." He said getting up and cleaning off the bones and scraps off his plate into the garbage. I looked at him and continued eating my food. He washed out the plate, fork, and cup and went back upstairs. I just didn't get it. Here I was trying to find out what was going on with him and he gets upset. This was why he was his father's child. I grabbed the remote off the counter cutting on my flat screen that I had installed on the wall in the kitchen turning it to The Real House Wives of Atlanta, finishing my food.

CHAPTER FIVE

MARTICE

"Chile, what you need to do is get your ass out of your mama's house. You twenty-two years old." I sat listening to Treyshawn tell me how it was just time, and getting my own place would be the best thing for me.

"Oh, believe you me, I'm working on it." I said cutting on the TV for the Real Housewives of Atlanta.

"Chile, your mama is a trip, but that's what I did when mine started nagging. I got my ass out and got my own place."

I thought about what he was saying and it was making sense. My mother just was not listening to anything I had said to her while we were eating. She's always putting Marquise on a pedestal like he was her Messiah, but me, she treated like a red-headed step child. She questioned about why we had no relationship, well there you go, she was too damn controlling. And far as church, well I attended but I just wasn't as dedicated as I used to be. My brother was the youth pastor and she sung in the choir. Powerhouse was her life, I grew up and now it just wasn't as important to me as it used to be. Not God, but the church itself.

"Yeah, well I'm trying to move out within the next few months, maybe right after her birthday." I said.

"She ain't about to let you go nowhere, watch! She controls you and your brother, and why she ain't got no man?" He asked.

"Your guess is as good as mine. She has not dated since my daddy passed." I said.

"Miss Marilyn needs a man, honey. So she can get off your back." He said.

I laughed. "Well my brother is not going to let that happen, he's too over protective of my mom." I said.

"Bullshit! You just watch. If he's datin' that girl from y'all church and she interfering, I bet your brother try to find her a man." Treyshawn said.

"Gurl, if I don't before him." I added.

"Yeah…" Treyshawn began to say.

I saw my brother's name and number come across my phone screen. "Hold on" I said to Treyshawn interrupting him as I clicked over.

"What's up?" I said.

"Before I come in and go to sleep did you want anything from Jewels? I'm stopping there to get stuff for my lunch this week and just thought I would hit your line and see if you needed anything." He said.

One thing was certain, me and my brother were different, but we could always count on each other; whether it was just a run to the grocery store or gas to put in each other's cars.

"Naw, I'm okay." I said but I paused and asked him, "Are you thinking about moving out soon?"

"Yep! Just as soon as I get these next checks from work. I've been saving and I almost have enough saved for a security deposit and furniture." He said surely.

I was so proud of my big brother. He had his plan already set. I just had to get off my ass and do the same thing, and as long as I was living here with my mother I would be forced to live like I was a little kid. It was her house and her rules, no matter how old I would get.

"Tice, can I ask you something?" I heard my brother say after a thirty second pause over the phone, which peaked my curiosity because he just came out of nowhere with it.

"Wassup?" I said listening.

"Is there somethin' that maybe you not tellin' mama that you wanna tell me?" He said.

I paused for a second. I knew that the questions were going to start. I knew that my mother had more than likely been confiding in my brother to find out personal information on me since me and her were not as close as her and him were. I just did not feel like dealing with this right now, not at the moment. And even if I did let my brother know I was gay I did not need him condemning me to hell like most pastors would anyway because he would not understand. I did not choose to be gay, this is what chose me, so as long as I could hide it from him and our mother then I would.

"No, why would you ask me that?" My response was quick but with a *now the ball is back in your court* sense.

"Oh just wanted to know. It just seems like maybe you need to talk about something. You know being in the ministry I can sometimes pick up on things little bro. So it's just that spiritual sense in me." He said.

"That's cool, Quise, but I have my friend on the other line." I quickly said so I could get him off the phone; if Treyshawn did not already hang up.

"Aw, my bad, see you in a minute." He said and I clicked over.

"You must think my name *EnVogue*, bitch." I heard Treyshawn say nastily in the phone.

"Shut up! My brother was on the other line." I said.

"Well damn, let me know something. Shit, I almost hung up, but anyways we going to Hydrate next weekend, honey, so be ready."

Now, Treyshawn knew damn well I did not fuck with club Hydrate. "Why we gotta go there?" I asked.

"Girl, just find a nice fit and let's go. Always asking fuckin' questions." He said irritated.

"Whatever. You know how I feel about the Hydrate on a Saturday night." I said.

"And so what. We only gonna be there for a few minutes, damn!" He said as if I knew. I could not handle the argument anymore I told him goodnight and that I would talk to him later.

CHAPTER SIX

MARQUISE

Once I dropped Isis off at her house, then went to the store, I came home took a shower, went to my room, texted Isis goodnight, and got in my bed. Work and school were both a few hours ahead and I had to get enough sleep to tackle both. My mind drifted to how soon I would be in my own spot and graduating from college in May, which was all I thought about nowadays. Being on my own, it would definitely give me the feeling that I was a grown man and not a little boy still stuck in my mother's house. I did not know how she was going to take the news since it seemed like she was so opposed to me moving out, but she definitely would understand after time. I was twenty-four years old and for most guys my age I had accomplished a lot. My phone started singing Mint Condition's "Someone to Love" which let me know that Isis was texting me back.

"You sleep?" Was her text, I responded with "No." After five minutes had passed, she Facetimed me. I answered and she was already smiling once she saw my face on the screen. "Wassup?" I said sitting up a little in my bed.

"Could not sleep, either." She said brushing her hair in her mirror and tying it up.

"I'm just really thinking about the move that I am going to make soon and also telling my mother." I said.

Well, I am sure she will be understanding about it. My granddaddy is the same way but it's just them being the parents that they are." She said.

Bishop Winston and First Lady Robyn both raised Isis because her parents died in a plane crash when we were twelve. It was a big blow to Isis, Bishop, and First Lady as well as the church. Isis' mother was Bishop and First Lady's only daughter. Theresa, who sung in the Voices with my mom, was also the director of the children's choir at the church until she passed.

"Yeah, well I'm a grown man - time for me to move out. My mother has to let the hold that she has on me and my brother go, now." I said thinking about how she told me that I was not ready to move out yet when I first told her about it. Her response was that so many things had to happen so that I could move out comfortably and be okay. To me that made no sense at all, and I could not understand why she was so opposed to me moving out and getting my own place like the responsible grown man that I was.

"Well she just probably will miss you." Isis said smiling at me.

"And I will miss here as well but I'm a grown man living under my mother's roof -those days are over for me." I said.

"Well I heard that." Isis said.

I looked at the clock on my wall it was12:30 AM.

"Well, bae, I'm sleepy and I have to be up in about six hours." I said yawning.

"Yeah, me too." She said pulling her covers back and getting in her bed. She pulled the covers towards her and blew me a kiss. At that point, I told her I loved her and I would talk to her later on and we ended the video chat. Putting my phone on the charger, I smiled thinking that once I got the apartment, the marriage proposal was next for us. I just knew Isis Stephens was going to be my wife, and soon everyone including her would know that.

CHAPTER SEVEN

MARILYN

Walking back to my office from going to McDonald's on my lunch break, my sister, Marian, was on my phone rambling about our mother.

"You know your mother is something else, who is she staying with when she comes for Easter?" She asked as I turned the key into my office door walking in and setting down my purse, phone, and McDonald's bag, with my southwest grilled chicken salad and bottle of water in it on my desk.

"She said she was staying at a hotel because she did not want to stay with neither of us." I said.

"That's crazy, why would she spend money. She can stay with me and I know you wouldn't mind." She said.

I took off my fur coat, hung it up, sat down at my desk, took out my hand sanitizer and squeezed a little in my hands rubbing them together, then I started going through the bag taking the salad and bottle of water out.

"Well let her stay in a room. She probably has a friend coming with her." I said.

"Marilyn, you know mama ain't traveling with no man." She said and I laughed.

Our mother and father were married for thirteen years before they divorced, and he moved into his own apartment. Their relationship was a constant argue over any and everything, they disagreed on every situation. My mother said I am just like my father when it comes to debating back and forth and not leaving things alone when it's really nothing to argue about in the first place. Five years after they divorced, my father passed of a massive heart attack at the age of 45. He worked for the railroad and lots of times he was stressed and had to watch the things that he would eat. My mother took it hard for a while, but she made peace with it and God, then she moved to California. My father sometimes attended Powerhouse with us, but he was not a regular member. His philosophy was that you did not have to go to church to be a believer in God. He believed that if God was in your heart, then you were a believer.

"Marilyn, when are you going to tell the boys?" I heard Marian say which made my stomach drop because I knew exactly what she was talking about.

"I don't plan on it, Marian." I said.

"Marilyn! What! No you have got to tell them. You have went all these years without telling them, they are grown now." She yelled.

"Marian they do not need to know because it is not relevant." I responded.

"How so? Girl me and mama done already talked about this, she said this is gonna come back and bite you in the ass." I made a sigh noise because Marian was definitely getting on my last damn nerve, now. And the fact that her and my mother were sitting up talking about the shit was making me even more upset.

"Why are y'all discussing it?" I asked.

"Well we wasn't. But mama brought it up in our conversation by asking me have you told them, or when were you going to. She said she should have just went on and did it but you already told her them your kids and you will." Marian said and I mocked her.

45

"Listen and hear me for the last time, I don't feel ashamed nor bad for not telling my sons what they don't need to know in the first place. The last thing that needs to happen is for my household to be stirred up with the shit from my past. Only God and the grave will know what I have done; with the exception of you, mama, and Rick." I said taking the small mirror out of my desk drawer to make sure my makeup was okay and my hair was, too. A Managers Meeting was going on after my lunch was over in the Vice President's office.

"Well, long as you know what you doin', Marilyn." Marian said with a sarcastic tone in her voice.

"And sister I do." I said popping a mint in my mouth, then sanitizing my hands again, and cleaning up my mess throwing it in the garbage.

"Well let me get off this phone. I know your lunch is almost over, and I have to go pick up Latoya and Jermaine early from school." Marian said referring to her daughter and son, my niece and nephew, who were sixteen and fourteen years old, spoiled as hell, and attended private school.

"Okay, well call me later." I said.

"Bye." She responded and hung up.

I stared off into space for a second thinking about the conversation and how her and my mother were both on it for me to tell Marquise and Martice a secret that I have kept for years. I talked to God every night, and every night for the last twenty-five years I have asked him to forgive me for what I did, and the fact that I would never tell the boys so long as I lived.

CHAPTER EIGHT

MARTICE

The music blasted out of the speakers at Hydrate as I stood by the bar sipping my rum and coke. Like I said, I knew this shit was going to be popped. I did not know, for the life of me, why Treyshawn loved this club. It was the same sissies in here every Saturday night, doing the same thing, and if you were a new face in the place, then you were the target for their pickup lines and bullshit. Treyshawn was entertaining some six-foot-three, light-skinned dread head for the past twenty minutes. I watched as they talked, laughed, and finally Treyshawn took his phone out and took the guys number before he walked off toward the other side of the club. It looked like he was there with his friends as well. The guy had a banging ass body, I could tell that he worked out from the way his t-shirt and pants fit him.

"Chile, what's wrong with you?" He asked as he walked up to me.

"Nothin', you know how I feel about Hydrate." I responded.

"Chile, let that go, you better get in here and mingle. You up in here lookin' all good and shit, and honey, I would kill for your body." He said nudging me.

I worked out at least three to five times a week after work, add to that eating right and if I say so myself my physique was the shit.

"I ain't thinkin' about none of these late ass fags in here." I said looking around.

"I guess." Treyshawn responded twisting his lips into duck lips.

"Well, who was that guy you gave your number to?" I asked.

"Aw, that's Cortez. I ain't seen him since forever. All that's gonna be is a fuck, all he want is some ass." He said and I laughed.

"And I'm quite sure that you're gonna give it to him?" I asked.

"And you better know. I told him if he don't answer when I call after we leave he ain't got to worry about me being available later on." He said.

I shook my head. Most guys wanted to fuck in the gay lifestyle anyway, moving onto the next, this was the reason I was single. Don't get me wrong I hooked up every now and then myself, but I had not been in a relationship, yet. I saw Jamar and some other guy walking toward me and Treyshawn.

Treyshawn and Jamar greeted each other with hugs like they had not seen each other in years. Jamar looked me up and down and I returned the same gesture. He did not care for me, and I sure as hell could not stand his grand fake ass either. I continued to sip my drink as he started talking to Treyshawn. The guy that Jamar walked up with started staring at me really hard. I did not know if it was a *damn, you look good* stare, or *you the bitch my friend talked about before we came up in here* look. I just hope I did not have to beat nobody's ass up in here tonight.

"Treyshawn, this is Terrell." Jamar said as Terell and Treyshawn both said hello to each other. "And this is Martice." Jamar said with a corner side eye look.

I said hello to Terell and rolled my eyes at Jamar.

50

"Chile, I didn't think you was comin' out." Treyshawn said to Jamar.

"Honey, I wasn't, but hell it was nothin' else to do. So me and Terrell came to see what the kids were up to at Hydrate." Jamar said.

"I hear ya. Well let me grab me a drink from the bar. Treyshawn said excusing himself.

Jamar whispered something to Terell. He looked at me again and a grin formed on his face. Just like a fag to talk shit and not say it out loud.

"Tell Treyshawn I will catch up with her later." Jamar said as him and Terell walked away.

I acted like I didn't even hear that bitch. *Tell him your damn self*, I said in my head.

Five minutes later Treyshawn came back. "Where did Jamar and his friend go?" He asked.

"I don't know and don't give a damn." I said.

"Honey, what's wrong with you?" Treyshawn said giving me the stank face.

"Girl, you know I don't like that bitch, and she asking me to beat her ass." I said as loud as I could over the music. Sometimes I hated using the gay lingo of girl, bitch, chile, and her but it was appropriate for a bitch like Jamar. He really was the true definition of a late ass fag.

"Honey, let that shit go, Martice. Why do you let her get to you?" He said.

"I ain't thinkin about that bitch." I said sipping the last of my drink and throwing the cup in the can where we were standing nearest the wall from the dance floor. The DJ started spinning an old Trina cut and all the dance floor got crowded.

"Please, I'm not worried about her, but she did say somethin' about tell you that she would talk to you later." I said.

"I guess." Treyshawn said.

My eyes went to the entrance and I had to blink twice because I saw the most attractive dude out. He had to be about six-foot-two, light brown, whoever lined him up was definitely good with the clippers from his head to his beard. He had the nicest red lips and he was rocking a fitted polo, jeans, and a pair of new Jordan's on. He came in with a crew of seven other guys and they were looking good as well, and masculine. I could tell he was not feminine at all. In the lifestyle you had your real feminine dudes like Treyshawn and that bitch, Jamar. I would turn it off sometimes especially being around my mother and brother; I did not want to give them any signs. Or you had the masculine dude that you could not tell if he was gay or not. You had your bi-sexual men and I did not care for them either. To me you need to pick a side - you were either gay or straight. These guys were a disgrace to women and gay men, especially the ones who were out here having kids and then decided to be gay after that. Your ass knew you were gay when you were with that woman.

People started moving out of the way as the guy and his crew made their way through the club and up to the VIP section where the DJ was. The DJ, DJ Tony T, greeted the guy with a slap of the hand and a man hug. I just could not take my eyes off the guy. He was fine as hell I could tell he was Puerta Rican and Black mixed from the way the waves in his hair lined up from his cut.

"Girl, who you staring at?" Treyshawn asked me.

"Nobody." I said snapping out of my trance.

"Yeah, okay. Let me find out." He said giving me side eye.

"So let's hit Vonshay's next week." I said. Hydrate was boring and looking at the clock it was almost 3:30 AM which was good because I was ready to go home, take a shower, and get in the bed because I did tell my mother I was coming to church in the morning.

"Yeah, your spot." He said giving me a look.

I smiled, "And you know it." I said.

Out of nowhere, Jamar came running over to Treyshawn.

"Chileee, Andre in here." He said like a little girl, he was damn near red in the face.

"Where?" Treyshawn asked as Jamar pointing to the VIP section and yep, it was the guy I was staring at.

"You know I'm gonna go make my move. I've been tryin to get with Andre for a minute now, honey." Jamar said.

"Well, girl you better go get him, shit, before somebody else do. Andre know he fine." Treyshawn added.

It was like all the guys in here were trying to get Andre's attention but he was ignoring them. I could see why though, sissies could really be thirsty. Jamar went up to VIP and sat with Andre and started talking to him, the whole time I watched as if I was in the conversation with them. I came back to reality when the DJ said last call for alcohol.

"Chile, I know you ready so let's go." Treyshawn said, as he was the driver for the night.

We started making our way through the club going to the entrance, for some reason I just had to turn around one last time to see if I could even get a glimpse of the VIP section and Andre, knowing that it would probably be my last time seeing him. As I turned taking one last glance, I was surprise to find him staring right back at me. I blinked like a deer in head lights, as he nodded, and smiled at me.

CHAPTER NINE

MARILYN

"Mama, you know Easter Sunday is in two weeks. Are you still staying in a hotel?" It was a Saturday morning I was in my house robe, pajamas, and slippers with my hair rolled up talking to my mother on my house phone.

"Hell yes. You and Marian are not getting on my damn nerves." She answered back.

I shook my head. My mother could be over the top sometimes with her mouth and the things that she would say to me and my sister, but she was still our mother and I loved her dearly.

"But you know I'm gonna be so glad to see Bishop and Robyn when I get in town, just like old times." She added.

"I believe you. And what about me and Marian?" I asked.

"Shit, I talk to and see you two all the time when I decide to come up. You asking this as if I don't never see y'all." She said. I laughed knowing that struck a nerve with her.

"Well, I am on my way to the health club daughter dear, I will talk to you later." She said.

I told her bye and hung up the phone. Today was a lazy day for me although I did have a hair and nail appointment this afternoon.

I called Marian. "Hey, girl!" I said when she answered her cellphone after two rings.

"Girl, I'm in the store trying to grocery shop and it's the middle of the month so all the food stamp people are in here." She said disgusted.

Shaking my head at her comment, I told her to call me later and she said that she would. I cut on my DVD player and decided to watch one of the old Powerhouse Broadcasts from the 80's that our soundman Myron converted from a tape. Looking at the old sanctuary and how we packed out the choir stand brought back so many memories; including the Jerri Curl hairstyles. We were in our red robes singing "Magnify Him" by Myrna Summers. I loved that song and started to sing along with the lead Rayna Jones who sung alto. The church went up and there was not a person in their seat. I remember those days of being up there in those robes, hot with the lights beaming on us, thank God those day were done. Sam used to work us when he directed, especially on this song because it was fast and we drove it just like the choir that Myrna Summers sung with on the album she recorded it on. It got to the special where we were repeating "Praise him, Praise the Lord" and the congregation was on their feet clapping, bobbing their heads, moving side to side, some waved their hands in the air, and I even heard some Holy Ghost screams. Then some of the altos and sopranos started to go in and catch the spirit. If this ever happened, the ones who didn't would just move out the way and let those who were going in and falling out do their thing. Nobody wanted to get hit when them arms went to swinging and the shouting and screaming started. Usually an usher would come up to the choir stand and assist. Once one person caught the spirit it was usually a domino effect, then someone else, then another person, until half the choir stand and congregation were gone in the spirit. Mable playing that organ the way she did tore the church up.

Bishop came to the pastor's podium, stood for a second, smiled and said " Well! y'all might as well go head and praise him!" He turned and sat back down in the pastor's chair, and the church went into an uproar again as the Holy Ghost music started playing.

"Yes, Lord!" I said smiling, I saw my mother, me, and Marian on the soprano side on the second row standing and clapping to the beat of the music. It took about thirty minutes to calm the church down. Bishop came to the podium again to give his message, *This was from a 1989 broadcast*, I thought to myself. Martice came flying down the steps, on his way to work.

"See you later, mama." He said getting his keys off the table, putting on his coat and hat.

I gave him a grim look and said, "Next time make it to church on time. You know walking in at 12:30 pm and service is over at 1:30 pm is not OK. I shouldn't see that from the choir stand. If you weren't hanging out every Saturday night then maybe you could get to church on time like you used to." I gave him the once-over look.

Martice looked at me, smiled, then opened the door walking out and closing it. I shook my head, I just did not know what was going on with him but whatever it was I just hope that it would pass. I turned my attention as Bishop Winston yelled, "Tell the Lawd you need 'em to work on ya!

When he work on you, you gots to pray on! Cause the time won't be long! Sang choir!"

As he took his seat and Sam stood us up, Mable and the rest of the band started playing the tune of "Work on, Pray on" the remade version by Dr. Charles G. Hayes & The Cosmopolitan Church of Prayer Choir. I loved this song because the soprano and alto sections would bellow out the words when we broke off into three parts, singing with the tenors. We were recognized for having one of the most powerful soprano and alto sections in the city of Chicago over the years. We could scream and holler some notes. I picked up one of the tambourines that was in the soprano section and handed it to one of the tenors, who started beating it fast, as the choir repeated "shout". Sam went back and forth, up and down with his hands directing as we kept repeating and repeating "shout" with the congregation back on their feet, yelling and encouraging us as we sung. This was one of those power filled broadcast services we had back then. You would get that every now and then where the spirit really showed up in the place. Once it ended, I cut the DVD off and decided to get myself dressed and ready for my hair appointment in a couple of hours.

JEFFERY ROSHELL

CHAPTER TEN

MARTICE

"Chile, you have got to enter that contest going on at Hydrate next Saturday night." Treyshawn said as I sat talking to him on my lunch break from work. It seemed like noon came around real quick this Saturday at the call center. I worked for a third party biller for Capital One's delinquent credit card accounts.

"Now you know how I feel about Hydrate." I said with an attitude.

"Yea girl, but that contest is for five-hundred-dollars, Tice! I know with one of your dance routines you would kill. Girl, just do it!" He said giving me attitude back.

I loved to dance it was a passion for me. It was only at Hydrate that I hugged the wall. Any other club that Treyshawn and I would go to I would be on the floor killing it.

"So what's the info on it?" I asked him.

"Girl, five-hundred-dollars to the best dance routine. Kevin, the club owner, just posted it about an hour ago on Facebook. He said that he closing it out today at 2pm, so chile you need to call like asap!" Treyshawn said with great excitement – I could tell he was smiling.

As I thought about it, I realized I could use the money. *I promised my mother I was going to Easter Service the following Sunday, plus my nana (grandmother) would be here. I could use the winnings to purchase a nice three-hundred-dollar suit and get some two-hundred-dollar shoes*, I thought to myself. That could be a perfect way to impress mama and nana.

"Call Kevin and tell him I'm in." I said as Treyshawn yelled at the top of his lungs. I shook my head and turned the volume down on my phone just a little.

"Hold on!" I heard him say as he clicked over to make it a three-way call. I heard the phone ringing when he clicked back over and by the fourth ring Kevin answered.

"Kevin, chile this Trey, go ahead and put my bitch, Martice Johnson, in. Honey, she gonna let the kids have it, and I mean literally have it, on next Saturday!" Treyshawn said and laughed.

I chimed in when I heard Kevin asked how my name was spelled and happily spelled it for him. He told me that the routine had to be no more than ten minutes, and to be at Hydrate no later than 1am because the competition was going to start at 2am. I told him okay, gave him my phone number so that he could text me Thursday evening of next week just to make sure that I was still in. Then Treyshawn and I both told him goodbye with Treyshawn hanging up the other line.

"Tice, you gonna kill it, girl. I already know." Treyshawn said.

"We will see, but let me get back on the phones. I got another two and a half hours here and then home so we can go out and kick it tonight." I said to him.

"Where we going tonight? To ole bump ass Glam Beats?" He asked me.

"And ya know it!" I said all excited putting my garbage from the turkey sub on wheat from Subway, a bag of plain Baked Lays, and a bottle of water I had for lunch in the trash.

"Well just promise me one thing if you do win?" I heard Treyshawn say as I was about to tell him goodbye and hang up the line to get back on the floor and on the phones.

"What's that?" I asked.

"That when you win that money, honey, you dish me a nice $250.00!"

CHAPTER ELEVEN

MARQUISE

Isis and I approached The Westyn Apartment Complex that was about ten minutes away from my home in the Evergreen Park/Beverly Neighborhood that my mother, brother and me lived in. The complex was very nice, but there were no vacancies for apartments in the area, so Westyn was my last hope to stay in the area. The Westyn Apartments had just been completed a year ago, so not only was that area very nice, those apartments were too. I parked my car in front of the leasing building.

"So this is it, huh?" Isis asked.

"Yeah…" I said as we both got out and started walking to the door. I opened it for her and we walked to the front desk where a heavy-set, blonde-haired woman with a name badge displaying "Kristie" sat.

"Hello!" She said looking up at the both of us.

"Hello, I'm Marquise Johnson." I said with a grin.

"Oh yes, Mr. Johnson I am expecting you for a tour today at 3pm. Please, you guys have a seat and let me get an application for you to fill out. There is also a $35 fee for credit and background check." She said handing me the application on a clipboard with a pen.

I handed her a twenty-dollar bill, a ten-dollar bill, and a five-dollar bill. I did not feel like writing a check, and besides I had the cash in my wallet. Having cash on hand always comes in handy for eating, as I frequently raid the lunch food trucks or the vending machines at work – I always seem to make sure that I have tens, fives, and singles on me. It took me ten minutes to fill out the application; Isis talked me through it, too. Once I was done I handed the app with the clipboard and pen back to Kristie. She looked it over and sat it down in an empty spot on her desk.

"I just need copies your paystubs and your I.D please." She said. I handed that to her and she paper

clipped everything together with my filled out application.
"Okay, so let's go take a tour!" Kristie said pleasantly.

Isis and I followed her out the door to one of the newly
built complexes; which was definitely me, peaceful and quiet
- not a sound. The lawn was cut nicely, too, which made The
Westyn Apartments look very upscale. Kristie took us into
building D121.

"So far there are only two families and another tenant
in a one-bedroom here, it's very quiet and there is a noise
ordinance for the building." She said as we walked down a
long, grey, carpeted hallway, the building had the new smell
still in it.

"I am going to show you this one here." Kristie said as
we stopped in front of door #34. As Kristie opened the door
she held it for me and Isis to go in, Isis mouth dropped and
my eyes damn near popped out of my head, this apartment
was beautiful and very spacious with a front patio.

"This is a two-bedroom and it is going for $875.00
That Includes your water, sewage, garbage, heat, and
central-air in the summer. Your light and gas are your
responsibility. Now let's take a tour of the two bedrooms, first
the master bedroom, then the other bedroom and bathroom."
She said as she closed the door and we followed her into the
living room and down the hall.

The master bedroom was very spacious and had a walk-in closet. The other room was just as nice and had enough space in it – I was thinking that maybe I could put in my treadmill and weight bench, with a desk to work off my laptop, along with a printer/scanner in it. I was already making plans for the apartment and Kristie hadn't even let me know whether I had the apartment of not, but I already claimed it so it was mine. Kristie led me and Isis back pass the living-room, toward the kitchen that had a nice dishwasher and stainless steel appliances in it and out the door as she locked it.

"The washer/dryer facility is in the other building. We have a total of 20 washers and 20 dryers in the laundry area for use. The parking is free but if you have guest you must remind them to park in the back of the parking lot in visitor parking so they won't get towed. Overall this is Westyn, so what do you think?" Kristie said as we walked back to the leasing office.

"I love it!" I said enthusiastically.

"Ma'am what about you?" Kristie turned and asked Isis. "Mr. Johnson seems to be doing all of the talking. Are you not pleased with your husband's choice?" Kristie said as Isis gave her a crazy look and I laughed.

"We are not married" Isis said with a smile.

"Oh I'm sorry, please forgive me." Kristie said.

"No, no apologizes needed. But when things are spoken…" I said looking at Isis grinning implying our future and she looked at me, smiled, and shook her head.

"Well maybe someday. And when that day comes and if you are living in Westyn I want an invite!" Kristie said smiling as she opened the door for us to go back into the leasing office.

We sat down and talked more about the apartment complex. I told her that I was definitely interested and wanted her to process my application right away for a move in by the end of the month of May, which was the perfect time for me to get everything together and be out of my mom's house right after graduation.

CHAPTER TWELVE

MARILYN

It was Thursday evening, 8:30pm to be exact, and choir rehearsal had started thirty minutes ago. I had already informed Solomon that I was going to be late tonight. I walked into the sanctuary, the band was playing and the choir was already standing up in the choir stand rehearsing with Solomon directing - all 100 members were present. Everyone was in high anticipation as Easter Sunday was the Sunday after next and the CD release concert was three months away.

"Altos, y'all a little flat tonight. What's goin' on?" Solomon asked them as I sat in the front pew. He smiled at me and told me it was ok to come on up to my section. Which I thankfully did walking to the soprano section sitting in my seat on the first row. All the strong altos, sopranos, and tenors sat on the first row of each section.

"Let's do it again. Here we go!" He said snapping his fingers and extending his hand up as they screamed out their notes. The sopranos and tenors cheered them on with claps and some said "Go head altos!" I sat my purse and coat down under the seat and stood waiting for Solomon to turn his attention to the soprano section as he made his way rightward in the pulpit moving from the altos, then to the tenors, then it would be to the soprano section. As I was waiting on Solomon I got a text from Marquise asking me, "Where the rest of the stuffed peppers were from yesterday night I had made?"

I replied back "Martice probably ate them since you didn't come in last night and eat them."

"Man!" Was his reply as I grinned and sat the phone down. My stuffed peppers were good if I'd say so myself. I stuffed them with shredded cheddar and seasoned ground turkey meat.

"Sopranos…" Solomon said approaching our section of thirty members. "Give it to me like y'all do from the gut!" He yelled patting his stomach with both hands as he raised his hand up in the air and we hit the note.

"That's alright Sopranos!" Some of the altos and tenors said as we all smiled.

"Oh we got this!" Marsha Davis said from the third row of the soprano section snapping her fingers and everyone laughed.

After about five more songs it was 9:30pm and rehearsal was over like clockwork. Solomon talked about the CD release concert and who are special guests were going to be. He also spoke about the uniform for the upcoming Sunday, which would be our purple robes with the black overlay. There was no rehearsal next Thursday night due to Easter weekend the following Sunday, but we were to be in our white robes with red overlay. We had three main choir robes we wore throughout the year until choir anniversary time. We would always get a new robe to add to the other additions instead of going out and buying an outfit, which I had no problem with.

If we were in a uniform it would be all black or all white including the shoes, which ladies wore heels, not flat shoes at any time. Solomon's wife Reeva, who was a first row alto, spoke about the women's day choir in May which she was over and directed. Reeva was very pretty, she was slender with long, jet-black hair resembling the actress Gabrielle Union a bit, she had just turned thirty-nine last month and did not look a day over twenty-nine. Reeva and

Solomon's daughter, Maria, looked like Reeva's little sister instead of their sixteen-year-old child.

And then we have Sam, Solomon's father whom the torch was passed from (he sits in our rehearsals as the choir chaplain). If we get to out of control he will stand up and yell, "Voices bring it down!" Memories of when I was in high school singing with the Voices and Sam was the Minister of Music would run across my brain every so often. We were a very powerful choir now, but nothing compared to the old voices from back in the day, they set the tone for us today. Once I got home, I got settled and called to check on my mother to make sure she was okay. I took a shower, read my Bible, prayed, drank a small cup of cranberry juice, got up under the covers and closed my eyes. My mind went to Rick and his last words to me before he passed on. I sat up, turned on my light and went into the closet. I dug way behind some boxes, shoes, and bags. I picked up a box that was behind a bag of clothes, opened it, and saw what I was looking for was still there. I immediately put the box and everything that was in the closet back in their places. Climbing back in the bed, I looked up at the ceiling in the dark; I had an almost sickening feeling to my stomach. "Jesus keep me near the cross!" I said out loud as I hit the button on my lamp cutting out the light, closing my eyes as sleep hit me clear dead on.

74

JEFFERY ROSHELL

CHAPTER THIRTEEN

MARTICE

I oiled down my chest and made it jump in the mirror as I waited for the guy on the microphone to call my name.

"Chile, you nervous?" Treyshawn asked me looking up from his cellphone, he had been texting somebody for the last ten minutes.

"NO... Well, yeah!" I said with a half-smile.

"Tice, you gonna kill, girl. Just give it all you got and don't let the crowd get to you! I'm telling you, you bout the best dancer in here tonight. I ain't seen no other good talent in here." He said.

I had to admit most of the performances here tonight were definitely elementary; nothing stood out to say okay I had to really bring it. Kevin, the club promoter, walked into the dressing room where I was to let me know that I was next. I stood up and glanced at myself one last time in the mirror. Treyshawn walked up behind me standing in the mirror. "If you was not my friend, honeyyyyy…" He said with a smile.

"What???" I said"

"Well, chile, you my sister." He said backtracking.

"And the feeling is mutual. I don't look at your ass like that either, honey" I said with a reassuring look.

Treyshawn laughed and said "Come on they calling you."

Kevin came flying through the doors letting us know it was time for me to go the stage. I looked in the mirror one more time at myself. I had on a pair of white fitted shorts, white K-Swiss shoes with no-show white ankle socks, a fitted baseball cap, and a chain. Damn, I was definitely looking good to go and ready to kill this dance routine. My chiseled muscled up body definitely showed my four-to-five times a week workouts I did at the gym. I walked down the long hallway to the stage, the curtain was still closed, but I could feel the presence of the crowd behind it. Treyshawn told me good luck as he walked off the stage and out to the crowd of people to watch the show I was about to put on. I closed my eyes and lowered my head as I heard the MC announce my name and the song I was about to preform to which was Tweets "Boogie 2nite". As the music came through the speakers and the curtain opened and the lights dropped on me. I danced and moved my body along to the music. Everything that had me nervous about preforming left me as I let the music do the talking and my body flowed along. I dipped down and dropped my booty to the floor making it twerk a little as the crowd went crazy shouting and encouraging me to go head. As the song ended I dropped down to the floor with my head bowed out of breathe. The crowd gave me a loud applause along with cheers and yells. Treyshawn came back up on the stage and we hugged each other.

"Chile, I told you, you was gonna kill that shit!" He said just as excited as I was.

"I was a little nervous, but I just let go and did what I do best!" I said walking back toward the dressing room. The one thing that I was happy about was that there was a bathroom with a stand in shower that I could use so that I could change and get cleaned up. I had sweated up a storm under those hot bright lights.

"Chile, where you wanna go when we leave here? White Castles or McDonalds?" Treyshawn asked sitting down on the couch.

"Let's go to White Castle. I want some chicken rings." I said grabbing my bag and going to the bathroom to shower and get ready.

"And the winner of tonight's dance competition is........."

"Martice, Boogie2nite!!!!" The MC yelled out and me and Treyshawn jumped up and down and hugged each other from the table by the bar where we were sitting. I walked through the crowd and up to the stage to get the money. I saw Jamar in the crowd looking at me like I had just killed his dog. I smiled at that bitch; even he could not get me upset right now - I just won five-hundred dollars!! I shook Kevin's hand, took a picture with him, and took the envelope with the money in it from him. I walked back to the table, Treyshawn had bought me a drink, it was sitting on the table waiting for me in front of my chair.

"Rum and Coke on me, honey!!" He said.

"Aw, thanks!" I said drinking it with the straw, sitting down in front of him at the table.

"Well this shit will be dying out pretty soon." He said. I downed the rest of the drink and threw the cup in the trash.

79

"I saw your lil' friend when I was walking to the stage to get the money" I said rolling my eyes.

"Who Jamar?" Treyshawn asked laughing.

"Yes, lookin' mad as hell. I wanted to say, girl pipe down it ain't always about your stuck-up ass." I said shaking my head. Treyshawn fell back laughing.

"Chile, he is really mad, huh?" Treyshawn said.

"And I don't know why, but that's your friend I don't fuck with him." I said.

Treyshawn downed the rest of his drink, instantly his eye's got big like he seen a ghost. I gave him a look, then turned around, standing behind me looking good as hell was the Andre dude. He had a fitted black sweater and blue jeans, a pair of fresh clean black and white Jordan's, and he was bathed in Burberry Cologne. I wanted to literally piss and shit on myself. Since the last time when I first seen him, all I could think about was when he smiled at me when me and Treyshawn was leaving the club. And now he was standing in my face smiling.

"I just wanted to congratulate you on tonight. You really did the damn thing on the stage." He said.

"Thanks!" I said turning bright red. Treyshawn obviously noticed because he cleared his throat and shook his head smiling.

"No problem. I'm Andre but most people call me Dre" He said.

"Martice." I said.

"Cool you hanging here for a bit before it closes or y'all getting ready to bounce?" He asked. I could not stop looking him up and down. Damn he was hot!

"Well actually we about to bounce it is getting late." Treyshawn said looking at us both from one to the other, then giving me the look like, *Chile, if you don't get his number so we can leave.* It was hitting 3am almost and I was tired from the competition a little, but I first had to get my chicken rings with honey mustard sauce in my system before I hit the bed.

"Well we're actually…" I couldn't finish because Treyshawn cut me off.

"Andre that child's number is 773-990-5555." Treyshawn said with an attitude giving me the bitch it's time to go, not spark up a conversation look.

Now any other time this hoe loved to shut the club down, but now his ass was ready to go home. Treyshawn was definitely a true Virgo. If it wasn't about them, they couldn't care less. I looked at him and shook my head. Andre took his phone out of his pocket, looked at me, smiled and said "What is your number again?" I gave it to him, he called me to make sure it was the right number and that I had his.

"Well, Martice, can you text me and let me know you got in okay after you and your homeboy get to the crib?"

"I sure will!" I said still with a smile. Andre walked back through the crowd more than likely back to the V.I.P Section.

"Chile, let's go!" Treyshawn said getting up and walking toward the door. I grabbed my bag and followed behind him as we exited the club. Treyshawn got into his 2013 grey Monte Carlo and I got in right behind him. He started the car up and began pulling off.

"I cannot believe Andre gave me his number!" I said all happy and shit.

"Chile, calm down, you get one number and your ass go overboard." Treyshawn said changing his radio station to 92.3 and stopping at the red light.

"Honey, what's wrong with you?" I asked turning my face up at him.

"Nothin, but damn you acting really thirsty calm down. Andre always in somebody face every week." He said giving me the *slow down you ain't even talked to him on the phone, yet* look.

"You sound a little mad." I said giving him a look. I was not for his bullshit right now because nobody paid him any attention tonight at the club. Every now and then he would get like this and be in a bitchy mood.

"Well I'm not, but take it easy, honey. Andre is not one to get serious with okay?" He said giving a look out the side of his eye as he got onto the Dan Ryan Expressway to go out to the Southside where we both stayed.

I mumbled "whatever" to myself and sat back in the passenger seat. Although Andre was very attractive, him being a regular at Hydrate, I knew he had a lot of the sissies in his face every weekend. I, for one, was not about to be no side piece, or even a jump off so that he could say he fucked me and was done. We pulled up into White Castles parking lot and Treyshawn ordered my chicken rings with fries, and got him some cheese sticks and a large vanilla shake.

"And let me just set the record straight. I am never hating, you are like my brother, Tice. I just don't want no game ran on you okay. Andre likes attention, honey!" Treyshawn said handing the lady a solid twenty that I handed to him from my wallet. She handed him our food and he handed me the bags and sped off.

"I know. It just kinda felt like you were hatin' though." I said looking out the window, Treyshawn made a sigh noise, shook his head, and kept driving. I looked at my phone because the screen lit up and it said I had a text message. It was Andre asking if I had made it home yet.

My text response was "almost" as I smiled looking out the window.

"Well enjoy it while you can." Treyshawn said.

He pulled up to my house about twenty minutes later. We said our goodbyes and I told him that I would call him sometime later today. I opened the door, cut the alarm off, then back to stay, made sure the door was locked, and quietly walked up the stairs to my room. I did not want to wake my mother because she had a tendency to come flying out of her room to yell and talk shit to me if I woke her up out of her sleep from coming in from the club. I laid my bag down on the floor, threw off my clothes changing into a pair of shorts and a t-shirt, laid my phone on my dresser next to my bed, and got under the covers. Before I closed my eyes I remembered that Andre told me to call him before I went to sleep. But, before I could, my phone was already lighting up with a text message - well two came through at the same time. One was from Treyshawn telling me that he had made it home and the other was from Andre saying, "Hey, did you make it home?"

"Yes. I was just about to text you." I replied back to Andre.

"Well. If it's possible maybe we can sit down and do lunch or something this week? My treat." Andrew replied. I smiled and already liked his style.

I typed into the message box, "That sounds like a plan to me".

After a minute of waiting he responded with "Okay, and that he would text me later today."

"Goodnite!" with a smiley face was the response that I gave him. I placed my phone on the dresser; it was at 93 percent battery charged so I highly doubt that it would need to be charged by the morning since I was going to sleep. I was happy that two things happened to me today, I won the dance contest for five-hundred-dollars, and also I got the chance to exchange numbers with Andre. That made me too excited all at one time. I closed my eyes to get what sleep I could. It was already Sunday, my mother would be getting up soon to make breakfast, but right now I could not take my mind off of Andre and how excited I was about talking to him later on today.

CHAPTER FOURTEEN

MARQUISE

I arrived on time to Midway Airport to pick my grand-nana up from her 4:00pm flight that was coming in from LAX in about thirty minutes. I was really excited to see her, it had been about six months since the last time she came home to Chicago. It was just a few days that passed since I filled out the apartment application and I was still waiting to hear back from Kristie and The Westyn Apartments. I was sitting on cloud ten, and I couldn't help but get excited that I would finally have my own place and be out on my own. My phone starting ringing, I looked at the stereo system and saw my mother's phone number come across the screen.

"Hey." I said.

"Is she here yet?" My mother asked.

"Not yet, almost." I said looking at the time on my clock.

"Well call me when she gets in the car." My mother said impatiently.

"A'ight, I will." I said ending the call. Soon after ending the call Isis texted me asking "What was I doing?"

I texted back and said, "Waiting on my granny at the airport. She's almost here." She told me to tell her that she said hi and to call her later when I was free. About ten minutes later, in the distance coming out of the doors was my granny with her bags. She had a huge red rollaway that she was walking with. For sixty-two, my granny looked to be no older than forty. I popped my trunk and got out of the car.

"Hey Baby!!" My granny said giving me a hug.

"How was the flight, granny?" I asked her picking up her rollaway and placing it and her other bag in my trunk and closing it.

"Good, good. Glad to be back in Chicago!" She said as she was getting into the passenger side of my car. I go into the driver's side and sped off onto Interstate 294-south.

"Have you told your mama you found an apartment yet?" She asked five minutes into our drive to the house.

"No, I figured I would break it over Easter Dinner, let it be a surprise, granny. I'm so excited about the place it looks real nice, but I have not heard back from the lady at the leasing office." I said with a little doubt in my voice as to whether or not I knew I would get the apartment. I was not under the impression that it took so long to let someone know whether or not they were approved.

"Claim it! You already got it!" She said looking at me like I already know what it is.

I smiled then my phone started ringing again.

"Damn, how many times she done already called you before I got off the plane?" My granny asked knowing it was my mom calling.

"Just once." I said laughing as I hit the button and before I could say hello my grandmother already answered.

"Yes, Marilyn!" Granny said annoyed.

"Hello mother, just wanted to make sure that you were off the plane and here. We have 5pm hair and nail appointments me, you, Marian and Latoya."

"Okay Marilyn, well I'm talking to Marquise, we should be pulling up shortly. Bye, Bye!" My granny said cutting my mother off and hitting the end button on the stereo system. I laughed out loud and got onto the I90 east ramp exit.

"Your mama will worry the skin off a damn dog, shit! Let me get here good first." My Granny said making a face and adjusting herself in the seat, I shook my head and continued to drive.

"Well I know one thing, I am ready to throw down on some greens with spice, macaroni and cheese, fried chicken wings, catfish, cornbread, potato salad, and my famous chocolate frosted yellow cakes!" She said smiling. I thought about all the food that she had just named. She was going to kick my mother immediately out the kitchen and go to work making all the food.

"Well, Granny, I'm looking forward to the food on Sunday" I said.

"And I always love to come home and cook for my grandbabies, even though your mama and auntie get on my last damn nerve!" She said shaking her head.

"Granny such language about your daughters" I said laughing.

"I'm sorry, pastor, they give me a headache." she said being funny. Ten minutes in and I was turning onto the 95th St. exit off the I57-south expressway, which meant there was only another fifteen minutes and we would be at the house.

There was a five minute pause and silence in the air before my granny broke it.

"Marquise, baby let me ask you something?" she said.

"Yeah." I said stopping at the red light.

"Do you ever think your brother might be gay?"

I damn near rear ended the car in front of me after hearing her ask me that question. The thought had crossed my mind before and Martice was definitely private with his personal life. Me nor my mother have seen any girls call, or come by to the house with or for him. I did not just want to come out and ask him, but my mother has dropped the ball in trying and find out what was going on with him lately. We were not really close as brothers. He did his thing and hung out with who he wanted to, and the same for me, we both led very different lives as adults. But I did not just want to come and accuse my brother of being a homosexual. I had my views on it, and the only thing that I would definitely do is pray for him.

"Granny I know Martice is very private, but I never want to make an assumption without the truth. But the same blood that saved me from gangbanging and running with the wrong crowd before I decided to fully give my life to God, is the same saving grace for him." I said stopping at another red light, it seemed like they were coming back to back.

JEFFERY ROSHELL

"Oh I'm not judging. Hell, my beautician at the shop in L.A. is gay and he hooks my damn head up all time. He's fun to be around, I just wanted to know what you might have been thinking. And Lord I wouldn't dare ask your mother!" She said as we both made a noise and laughed.

Funny as it might be, my mother was definitely not having that. If she even had a thought that Martice might be gay she would be all over him with a Bible and holy oil. She lived the Bible to a tee, and if you did not want to follow it and its doctrine, you had to leave her home. She already stayed on him for not regularly attending church. I was just glad I had a love for the church and God on my own. I had not always been the good Christian guy that I am now, I gangbanged, smoked weed, and even sold it. I slept with different girl after girl until I decided to become serious with Isis, moving her out of friendship territory and also getting myself right with the Lord.

As a child my mother always had me and Martice in church, but church did not live in me until I was called into the ministry at eighteen. I believe that happened when God spared me in a robbery attempt on the Westside of Chicago. I was selling a dime bag to a dude and he pulled out a .38 and told me to give everything I had to him. I didn't move quickly enough and he pulled the trigger, but it locked on him. He looked at me and took off running as if he knew I was about to kick his ass for doing that. Little did he know, if I was not in as much shock as I was at what happened, he sure enough would have gotten just that. He was three inches shorter than me in height and didn't appear to weigh no more than a hundred and fifty pounds. Singing was my saving grace as well, I was never a choir dude, but I sung with a group in high school. We used to tear the roof off the talent shows and the girls loved us. I went from doing that to singing solo. Isis told me that was my life's plan from God, that if I waited on him, he would definitely send a contract and a company to my doorstep with all the talent shows I was doing, and the free-lance singing at the karaoke bar "B-Low's" up the street from my house, every now and then.

"Well, he has not confirmed anything, granny, so we can't assume this is the case." I said pulling up in front of the house.

She looked at me and said, "Yeah, okay."

"I'm surprise your mama not in the window looking out like "Carrie" from the Stephen King book." Granny said as we pulled up to the house.

I laughed as we got out of the car and I started taking her bags out of the trunk. She grabbed a hold of the rollaway and we walked to the door and my mother opened it. They gave each other a quick hug and we all walked in the living room with me locking the front door behind me.

92

"Martice not here, yet?" Granny asked.

"He's on his way home from work." My mother responded.

"Cool, well pour me some juice or somethin', Marilyn, I'm thirsty." Granny said to my mother who went back into the kitchen to do just that.

I sat down and started texting Isis about tonight's plans with our friends, Kevin and Nicole. They were another young married couple from Powerhouse who we hung out with. We had so many similarities, we all were the same age and Kevin and Nicole were both the relationship leaders in the youth class. Isis responded with an "Okay, great" after reading the plans I left her. She then told me that she would be ready within an hour, which gave me enough time to shower and get ready as well.

Martice came flying through the door. I heard he and my granny embrace each other with a hug and how they both were happy to see each other. My mother came out of her room and spoke to Martice. She also let my granny know that my aunt, Marian, and my cousin, Latoya, were on their way so they could go to the beauty shop to get their hair and nails did for Easter service on Sunday. I looked at the time on my phone again, and decided that I needed to get a move on things. I looked at Martice as he walked back into the living room and then up the stairs, the whole time his face was in his phone texting, he was smiling from ear to ear. Whoever was texting my little brother had to be important because his face was bright, beet red.

CHAPTER FIFTEEN

MARILYN

Easter Service was packed to the max which was no surprise at Powerhouse. Between the fire, Holy Ghost message that Bishop gave, to The Voices singing "He Shall Feed His Flock", I knew that service was going to be spirit-filled which ended with Holy Ghost shouting. Dinner was at Marian's house, her husband Russell was in charge of grilling the chicken, fish, steak, and Italian sausage, it was just that warm out in April for anyone to be out barbequing today.

"I just want to say that I have enjoyed you all, but it is time for me to get back to Cali in the morning, but I love my daughters, son-in-law, and my grandbabies!" Mama said proposing a toast and everyone lifted their glass or cup in the air.

"Mama, we're always happy to have you fly home." Marian said.

"Granny, I want to come to L.A. for my graduation gift!" Latoya said.

My mother gave her a nasty look and then changed the subject, Latoya was fast as hell, and I'm sure she could not wait to get from under Russell and Marian to be in some boy, or even man's face, soon. I caught my mother's drift and chuckled a little bit, grabbed my glass and took a sip of my wine. We had a full course meal, mac and cheese, greens, cornbread, dressing, and potato salad to go along with the meat.

"I got some news!" Marquise said forking up some macaroni and drinking from his cup. Everyone including myself looked at him.

"I found an apartment!!" He said looking at me smiling as everyone said congratulations.

I made a fake smile and drunk some more wine.

"It's a really nice place and it has a lot of amenities! It's the Westyn Apartments!" Marquise said excitedly.

"Wow, nephew, my co-worker said those are pretty nice." Russell said.

"Unc, they are! Not to mention the area is very nice. I should be hearing from the leasing agent any day now." Marquise said.

I was not the least bit happy nor pleased with what the hell I was hearing. I told him he was not ready to move out, yet. I told him to wait a while. I just sat there phony faced because he was doing the exact opposite of what I told him to wait on doing.

"Well, bro, at least you're about to get out." Martice said looking at me out the side of his eye.

I looked at his ass like *shut the hell up, you wouldn't know the first thing about a move out, so why fix your mouth to say anything.* I just did not understand why Marquise was not giving this logical thought. He was only ready to move out just so he could say he finally moved out. What about all the things that go along with actually being responsible to take care of an apartment?

"Congrats, baby! I'm happy for you!" I said and to see the look on his face was priceless, like he just knew I was telling him a bold face ass lie. I poured myself another glass of wine, I was not about to let this ruin my spiritual high from church service that I was still on.

After dinner was over we had dessert, which was my mother's homemade chocolate cake and Marian had two types of ice creams to go along with the cakes - vanilla or mint chocolate chip. Once dessert was over, we all got ready to leave for home; Marquise was taking my mother to the airport in the morning and I had to get myself ready for work. Once I got home and said my good nights to my mother and Marian, I laid in the bed and thought about the news that Marquise had gave today. He was really getting ready to try and move out. I still knew for a fact, that no matter what anyone would say, he was not ready, in my eye sight, and to just sit back and let him make such a mistake would be beyond ridiculous. I said a silent prayer, and drifted off to sleep.

Monday rolled around and the work day was rather busy. Between being on the phone every five seconds with another client, helping to resolve health insurance bills, to other duties upper management kept calling my office for, I just wanted to go home, take a shower, eat, and then call it a day. I picked up my phone, quickly making a call I almost forgot about that I needed to make before I left to go home.

"Thank you for calling the Westyn Apartments, this is Kristie speaking how can I help you?"

"Hello Kristie, my name is Debra James and I recently heard that you're possibly renting to a soon to be ex-tenant of mine, Marquise Johnson?"

"Yes, Mr. Johnson has put in an application for renting from us." Kristie said with happiness in her voice.

"Well, before you get ready to make any decisions, I just wanted to give you a call and let you know what type of tenant Mr. Johnson is."

"Great, so tell me should Mr. Johnson be considered as a dynamic tenant for property here at Westyn?" Kristie asked eagerly.

I rolled my eyes signed and said, "No, Mr. Johnson was everything but a good tenant when I rented to him. And if you have a moment I just want to give you the full story on just why he wants to move from my property. He probably didn't list me down as his last landlord." I said.

Say whatever, but Marquise was not ready to move out. I was not ready for him to move out. And this was me only doing for him what a good mother would do for her son. He would thank me for the favor later on.

There was a silent pause before I heard Kristie say, "No, he did not mention that he was moving from another property at the time, so this, I would love to hear."

CHAPTER SIXTEEN

MARTICE

My first date with Andre was going to be everything. I had to make sure I had on a nice outfit, my teeth were brushed, breath was on point, and I smelled like a million bucks. I frequented the Bath and Body Works men's section from time to time because they had a decent selection, and it was cheaper than getting the more expensive fragrances from the mall from Macy's or Carson's, even the cologne stands could be pricey. I loved Bath and Body Works as well because of the Candle Barn store; my mother loved the candles and every July for her birthday I would get her four huge candles of different fragrances that she enjoyed, plus a two hundred dollar gift card so she could get her lotions and perfumes.

Andre picked me up in his 2011 black, Dodge Charger and we decided on Dixie Kitchen in Hyde Park. Daylight savings time had started a few weeks ago, so it was still light outside at 7pm. I enjoyed the scenery as I looked out the window as Andre bumped 92.3 on his stereo system.

"You quiet as hell." He said looking at me and smiling.

"Just enjoying the scenery, that's all." I responded looking at him.

"You don't get out much?" He asked me.

"Yeah, but usually it's to a club. I rarely get to go out on dates. This something I've wanted to do for a while." I said.

Thinking back on my last relationship it only lasted for a brief moment; when I really sit back and think about it I wouldn't call it much of a relationship. We were really only dating, I remember having to ask him where the "relationship" was going on several occasions. Truth be told, our relationship was mainly sexual and going to clubs together. Our last date was in 2013 to which he decided to move south suddenly; I haven't heard from him in two years. Since then, I have been doing me and making everything about me. I figured eventually I would meet someone, and well I think I have now.

Dixie Kitchen had a nice crowd for a Tuesday evening, which I'm not surprised because their food was known for being off the chain. After our short wait we were seated and our waitress, Tracy, introduced herself; she asked what she could start us off with and if we were having appetizers to go along with the meals. Andre ordered a beer and the jerk wings and greens meal, I had the baked tilapia with dirty rice and a Sprite.

"So, out of all the guys that are after you, why me?" I asked needing an answer to this question.

Andre sipped the beer that Tracy sat in front of him, looked at me, and said, "I'm generally not drawn to the ones who are thirsty, all they want is the dick from me." He said and I laughed.

"Well, you're not lying. Gays can sometimes be just like female hoes." I said sipping my drink.

"Yeah, I mean I love fucking, but it's more to it than just that, you know? Especially now that we kickin' it." He said smiling at me.

Damn, he looking good tonight with his fitted red shirt, smelling like a million bucks. I thought to myself as Tracy sat our meals in front of us. I asked for another Sprite and Andre ordered another beer.

"So do your people know about you?" He asked me.

"No." I said through a mouthful of the fish and rice.

"Good." Andre said. "I'm not into those real queenie ass gay dudes. If I brought you around my fam' I don't want them to question what the deal is with us." He continued as he was sipping the beer that Tracy sat in front of him.

"Yeah, I understand. I only date masculine, gay guys because of this. My mother is real heavy into the church and so is my older brother. He's the youth pastor at the church as well." I said.

I know I had my moments with Treyshawn, but I knew how to turn it on and turn it off, Treyshawn on the other hand did not give a damn. His family knew, and he said that he loved it that way because tip-toing around and lying about his life was something that he could not do. Maybe one day I would have that same attitude as well.

"Sounds like you got to really keep it on the hush, hush." Andre said.

"Yea, my mother does not play that, she's saved and sanctified." I said looking out the window for a second, then returning my attention to him. "Are you the only child?" I asked attempting to change the subject.

"No, I am the baby though. I have two older sisters who are thirty-four and thirty-six." He replied.

"And how old are you?" I asked.

"I'll be twenty-nine in September." He said nodding his head at me. I liked the fact that the conversation was going smoothly; these were the things you generally asked on a first date.

"A Virgo." I said smiling.

"Yes, sir! One of the best signs out." He replied.

"When is your birthday?" He asked.

"In December, I'm a sag. To correct you, Sagittarius is the best sign under the zodiac sign." I said rather proudly. Andre gave me a look, and then a smile formed on his face.

"Yea, y'all a'ight." He said as he was finishing his second beer and put the empty bottle on the table.

I could see that we had a few things in common, especially being the baby of our families. I just really could not believe the guy that every dude at the club wanted was on a date with me. My phone buzzed letting me know I had a text message it was my mother. "Where are you?" she texted. I rolled my eyes replied back that I would be home soon. She texted back and said, "Ok, don't stay out too late because I do not want to hear the door chime and the alarm while I'm in a deep sleep."

"Andre. Question." I said looking at him.

"Martice. Answer." He responded eating his food and staring me dead in the eyes.

"With all the attention that you're getting, how are you going explain to your fan base that you may be seriously seeing someone now?" I asked him.

"You got Facebook?" He asked me.

I looked at him with a puzzled expression as to what he was hinting at. "Yea, do you?" was my response.

Andre picked up his Samsung Galaxy. "So how do you spell your name, again?" He asked typing and looking at his phone screen. I spelled my name for him. "Alright. If you will, accept my friend request and add me." He said as I picked up my phone to see his request. I looked at his profile picture which was him blowing smoke circles out from the weed he was smoking. I hit the confirm button and we were friends.

"Cool, cool." He said looking at the phone and typing something. A minute after he finished he looked up at me and smiled.

"What?" I asked smiling just a little myself.

"Update your newsfeed." He said.

I gave him a crazy look and did just that. As I scrolled down to about five messages, I looked at Andre and smiled. He had posted, "Out to dinner wit the potential 'one'" with an emoji smiley face. His status update had already received sixty likes and twenty comments of "who?" within five minutes.

CHAPTER SEVENTEEN

MARQUISE

A week had passed before I finally received a letter in the mail from Kristie over at Westyn. I could not believe the letter I was reading, thanking me for coming in to view the property site, but unfortunately, Westyn would not be looking to rent to me. I just could not believe it.

"Damn, man!" I yelled balling my fist up and slamming it down on the desk in my room. I just did not understand, the conversation went rather well, I know for a fact my credit is A1, I have a score of 865. I sat down and laid my head back on my bed, I didn't know if I wanted to shed tears or just be numb.

Gathered my composure and said a prayer, "Lord, I don't question anything that you do, but I just want to know why? And I know the decisions that you make should not be questioned, but I had my heart banking on that apartment. Lord, I know you got a better plan for me and I will wait until you move in my favor. Thank you for what you have, will, and continue to do for me." I opened my eyes and moved on with my day.

I focused my attention on May 22nd, which was when I would be graduating Chicago State with a Bachelor's Degree in Information Technology. Also I kept my heart set on still planning to propose to Isis at the party after graduation. Isis was finishing her Nursing Degree at Prairie State College in Chicago Heights (a south-suburb outside of Chicago); she only had about a year and a half left before she would finish her degree program and take her state board exams. I texted my mother to let her know that I didn't get the apartment, she responded with a "Sorry, baby, something better will come later." I responded with, "Thanks, love ya."

I needed to take my mind off things and get out of the house. I was off today from work and did not have class so I grabbed my gym bag and decided to go do an hour of cardio and weight lifting at L.A. Fitness gym. I wasn't as ripped up as my little brother, but I definitely could put the work in on the weight bench. That's when the thought hit me to ask

Martice to come to the gym with me the next time I went to spot me. As I was thinking and walking down the steps, when I got to the door I thanked God for not blessing me with getting the apartment, for I definitely knew that better would be coming soon and very soon for me.

CHAPTER EIGHTEEN

MARILYN

Coming through the door, I dropped my Macy's, Carson's, Bath & Body Works bags, and my purse at the door. I turned and locked the door, picked up my bags and preceded to my room, laying everything on the bed. I saw a text message from my mother asking me to call her as soon as possible. As I dialed her the phone rang only once and she picked up without saying hello. It sounded like she was going off and I could tell she was talking to a police officer as well.

"They cleaned out everything in my garage, those bastards." She yelled into the phone.

"Mama, what happened? I asked her sitting down on the edge of my queen-size bed.

"You can't have shit! And it wasn't nobody but that trash that done moved in down the way. They standing outside lookin' like they don't know what happened. Hold on, Marilyn!" She said and I could hear her footsteps walking.

"I bet won't nobody bring they ass down here and take nothing else!!" I heard her yell then it sounded like a gun shot went off and I heard a scream.

"MAMA!" I yelled.

"Yea, I ain't playin' that shit, Marilyn. I bet won't nobody come down here and steal nothing out of my garage again. Let alone while I'm here at the house. Just as long as I got my girl, Dessa Rose, here." She said referring to her .45 that she had. This was a real shocker because my mother lived in Baldwin Hills, and even though it was right by Crenshaw, you rarely heard about anything in that area far as the robberies and murders.

" Hold on, again. The Channel Eight News is here!" She said. I dropped my jaw, and made a face. *Was it that serious for the newscasters to come by?* I thought.

"This is Slyvia Presbrooke with ABC Channel Eight News, we are at the home of Ethel Jenkins, whose garage was broken into and cleared of everything that she had. Now there has been a rash of break ends in the Baldwin Hills area within the past two weeks, and Ethel is the latest. Miss Ethel, ma'am, about how much and what did they take?"

"They took my damn four-hundred dollar lawnmower, my lawn chairs, my canopy, my eight- hundred- dollar, damn, grill I got from Brison's. Not to mention my James Brown and The JB's, my Patti Labelle, my Isley Brothers, and all my Motown tapes and records!!'" I heard my mother yell.

I could tell that the camera was right in her face, and I knew she was hot because growing up in the house all you heard was Marvin, Stevie, Diana and The Supremes, and Martha and The Vandellas on Saturday mornings when she would clean and then relax afterwards.

"Miss Ethel, what would you like to say to the individuals who broke into your garage have stolen all of your belonging out of it?" I heard the news lady ask my mother.

It got quiet, but I quickly heard her whisper to the camera man to zoom in on her, and then on queue I heard her spit out through gritted teeth, "Go get your ass a damn job!"

I heard the news lady say, "Live from Baldwin Hills, I'm Sylvia Presbooke, ABC News Channel Eight." Then she goes on to speak back to mama, "Thank you Miss Ethel, and I hope they find out who is doing this." She said as she wrapped up the interview.

"Who you tellin'? They better before I do, cause the next time, I got something for they ass!" Mama said. I could imagine that she was waving that damn gun.

"Alright, now, don't hurt nobody!" Sylvia said laughing.

"Honey, okay!" My mother added laughing, saying goodbye to Sylvia and then I could hear her going into her house and shutting the door.

She then told me everything that had happened. As I'm listening to her tell me the story, I heard loud music coming from outside the front.

"Mama, I'm going to call you back." She replied "ok" and I got up and walked to the living room to look out the front window by the door. There was a black, Dodge Charger with tinted windows and expensive rims sitting in front of my house. I turned up my nose wondering who it was and why did they have to park in front of my house of all places. I got the answer to that question when Martice got out of the passenger side. After thinking about it, that same car had been coming around here lately, I put two-and-two together realizing that the mysterious driver was for Martice. I began to wonder who was this he was hanging out with now? I watched him walk to the door, getting his key out. Before he could open the door, I had already opened it for him. I startled him, which sent a grin across my face.

"Who was that?" I asked as he walked passed me as he came through the door.

"That's my buddy from work." He said heading straight to the kitchen. Me being who I am, I was not about to let this go. With the frequency of this car coming around here, for it to be just a buddy from work they sure were really, really tight to hangout on off days.

"It's funny you never mentioned this buddy of yours before, and I have noticed that they've been coming around here a lot." I said looking at him.

"Mama, please, you're going to seriously argue with me about who I'm hanging out with? I'm twenty-two years old!" He said sarcastically, looking at me like I had lost my damn mind questioning him like I was.

"Yes! Because I don't know who's showing up at my door, your grandmother's garage got broken into today and she was on the local news in L.A. talking about it!" I said sitting down on the couch.

"What?! Is she okay?" He asked me coming out the kitchen with a cup in one hand and a bottle of grape juice in the other.

"Yes, she's alright, she made the news because there have been a rash of other robberies in the Baldwin Hills area lately. She has been the latest" I said.

"Well, that just goes to show it's not just happening here in Chicago." He said going back into the kitchen. That I had to agree with him on, all the time we were thinking that the high-time crime was going on here in Chicago, but it was all over the world.

"Granny will have all that they took brought back in no time." Martice said coming out of the kitchen hitting the steps. Before he could too far I went back to what I initially was questioning him about.

"So who is your friend?" I asked. Martice looked at me and made a face. He knew I was not going to let this go.

"His name is Andre, he just got on the team about a month ago and we hung out tonight. His girlfriend had a birthday party at Carraba's in Boilingbrook today." He said blinking as he spoke. When I heard the word girlfriend come off his lips I was immediately relieved. That's all I needed to hear, nothing more had to be said about who this person was picking him up and hanging out with him.

"Oh, one more thing!" I said as he turned again and looked at me. I smiled very big and happily, and then asked him, "So, did you see any girls you might be potentially interested in?"

CHAPTER NINTEEN

MARTICE

"My mama nosey as hell!" I said to Treyshawn as I laid across my bed and turned on my 32-inch flat screen TV that sat on the dresser facing my bed.

"Chile, what she ask you?" Treyshawn asked.

"Who Andre was and how did I know him, trying to find out tea." I said rolling my eyes. I knew making up the lie would keep her off my ass about why he kept picking me up from the house.

"Well, like I been told you, honey, it is time for you to move out of your mother's house. Your brother done found

him an apartment, girl, and it's time for you to do the same."
Treyshawn said.

I was listening to him, but I did not want to keep hearing the shit over and over. I knew that I needed to move out of my mother's house and get my own place. But right now with the job I had and the fact that I did not have a college degree, I needed find a plan b quick with the way prices for apartments were here in Chicago. Everything was so damn expensive.

"And have heard you, I am working on that." I said to him looking at my phone and seeing a text from Andre.

"Andre just texted me, girl, saying he had a good time." I said smiling.

"Andre really feeling you, girl. I saw that post that he put up on Facebook. I was like, damn, Tice really got him going. There has not been one to do that to Andre before." Treyshawn said.

"Well, I'm just taking it slow, but definitely feeling him as well. I haven't smiled like this in a minute." I said to Treyshawn as I was responding to Andre's text saying, "I did as well."

"Don't Andre got his own apartment?" Treyshawn asked.

"Yea, he does, he stays off 79th and Aberdeen." I said thinking about it. I had not been over there, yet, but he planned on inviting me soon to spend the night. That area was the notorious, Englewood Community of Chicago, so I was pretty skeptical about going over that way. You didn't know whether or not you would get shot and/or killed going through there. Andre told me that he grew up over there and everybody in the hood pretty much knew who he was.

"So, you still think that after what happened this evening that your mama doesn't know?" Treyshawn asked.

I smacked my lips and sighed. "Are we going there with this shit, again?" I asked.

"Chile, your mama know! You need to just come out and tell her you like boys. What the fuck is the big damn deal? So what, they don't accept you, it takes the burden off living a lie, Martice! And that's what you doin', living a damn lie!" Treyshawn yelled.

I was tired of hearing this shit; I was tired of him telling me what to do! Just because he did not give a damn about what his family thought and had the strength to tell them, at this moment right now, I was not ready to do all of that. And nobody was going to force me or make me feel bad about doing it. When I was ready, then I would be ready, and as long as I had that understanding with Andre, that was all that mattered to me.

120

"Look, just because you did it and it worked out for you doesn't mean it will for me. Know that everything does not work for everybody, Treyshawn! Like I said before, when I'm ready is when I tell everyone!" I yelled at him.

"Well do you! I'm just telling you, but I don't know how you can do it, It must be real complicated being you, honey!" He said trying to throw shade.

"Bitch, whatever!" I said changing the subject.

"Well get your panties out of your ass, honey. Call me later, I got company coming over and I need to get ready for them." Treyshawn said.

"I'm good. I know you're only looking out for me, but this is something that I have to do, and until I'm ready this is just how it's gonna be." I said.

"Well, you know what you doin', I promise this is my last time talking about the shit. You just do you, but make sure you making the right decision for you, and not just to keep your mama and brother off your ass. You can only make Martice happy." He said.

I was hearing him but once again, I did not want to hear what he was saying to me. "Talk to you later on." I said to him.

"Bye!" Was his response and then the line clicked.

CHAPTER TWENTY

MARQUISE

It was the second Sunday of May and I was up preaching a very powerful word that the Lord had blessed me with. I was sweating bullets, but I was hitting home on everything from the job market, to the killing going on in Chicago, to waiting patiently on God for your miracle, or whatever it might that was coming. I had everyone on their feet from the congregation to the choir stand, yelling and encouraging me to keep going on and preaching the truth.

"Cause without God on our side, my brothers and my sisters in Christ, we would be nothing without him! He is the One you look to, when that bill can't get paid; ladies, when that man walked out on you; brothers, when that woman walked out on you; when that job gave up on you; when you feel like all hope is gone; nobody there in the midnight hour to feel your pain! But Jeeesus is the answer for the world! Today I say Jeeesus will keep you when you feel like nobody else cares. Friends have turned their backs on you, look to Jesus he will be that friend until he gives you new friends to fill that void when those old fair-weather friends leave you behind.

"I tell you about how Jesus took me from the streets at eighteen, and gave me a vison to preach to the people! To teach the people about his Word! To encourage someone to let them know that what they are going through is only temporary."

I was all over the pulpit, and the congregation and choir was feeling the words that I was preaching and the emotion that I was putting into the sermon. I witnessed some of congregants catching the spirit as the Holy Ghost music started to play. Isaac, the organist, would play and then stop as I preached with high energy and low energy during the sermon. My mother would be my biggest supporter this morning, all I heard was her mouth and yells saying, "Say that Marquise, preach God's Word!"

"I say when you got God, you don't need to worry about whether or not that job is gonna come cause, He will!

He will! He will keep you! You don't have to worry about how them bills gonna get paid! Ooooh, Lawd!!" I belted out in the sermon. I felt the Holy Ghost as I continued, "I came not to give you a show, but to preach to you the unadulterated truth, for I know my God shall supply all your needs according to his works! Y'all don't hear me! I said, the man will give you peace of mind when the world is definitely on your shoulders!

"That's what the Word has spoken to me to put it in my spirit, Bishop!" I said turning toward Bishop Winston and the other associate pastors in the pulpit as they encouraged me with shouts and praises as they stood on their feet. I went from one side of the pulpit preaching the Word, to running toward the other side and doing the exact same thing. It was God's spirit that had taken over me, and I was on fire. My Mother continued to yell "Yes, Lord!! Preach!!" I got down on my knees as the congregation yelled and yelled, and the Holy Ghost screams from the ladies of the church started ringing louder and the Holy Ghost music started playing from the organ. I felt a towel being wrapped around my neck from one of the nurses who sat in the pulpit; she also wiped the top of my forehead with another towel. I got up off the floor and she handed me a glass full of cranberry juice, I drank it and thanked her.

I sat down in the seat and lowered my head, saying a silent prayer now that my sermon had come to a close. The other associate pastors gathered around me and prayed over me, something they did whenever Bishop or another pastor, or myself, finished their sermon.

"Well I tell you, when God comes in this place, He sho' 'nuff shows up!" Bishop said into the mic from the podium. The congregation took about another five to ten minutes to calm down from the high praise that went up from the sermon I gave. Bishop opened the doors of the church, and Solomon handed the mic to my mother and I heard the melody to Tramaine Hawkins' "Changed" playing softly on the organ. My mother started singing the solo part which I knew was going tear the church up again in praise.

"A wonderful change has come over me," the choir sang as my mother did her solo runs. There screams and shouts from women in the congregation, the ushers went over with tissue and fans to soothe and calm the Holy Ghost on them as it came into the atmosphere of the sanctuary again. My mother started to really feel the song, she walked down into the congregation and started singing to people about how God changed her and how so glad she was that he changed her walk, her talk, her heart, and how he changed everything about her. My mother handed the mic to Solomon as she cut a step back to the soprano section.

Some of her soprano sisters started catching the Holy Ghost and screaming as the organist played a Holy Ghost bump and everybody was on their feet in the sanctuary. God had really moved in this service, that for a minute, we seemed to have forgotten that the doors of the church were open. It was a blessing to see that eight new souls had come to give their lives to the Lord.

CHAPTER TWENTY-ONE

MARILYN

Monday came around speedily. The work day was going well and since I would be working until 7pm tonight, I decided to go home for lunch for two hours to relax. I knew Marquise and Martice were both at work, so I was looking forward to the quiet time and the opportunity to prepare dinner for the evening. I loved that my job and home was a short distance between one another - only thirty minutes - this left me plenty of time to multitask on my ride home. I called the salon to schedule a much needed touch up of my hair and nails for this coming Friday.

I dialed Marian's number but she was out getting some things together for a party they were giving Latoya for her birthday next Tuesday. As I was driving home I thought about my boys. It was almost time for Marquise's graduation ceremony. I smiled as I thought about the outfit that I would be wearing. The blue suit and matching Sunday-hat I picked up from Carson's last weekend was exactly what I had needed to make a grand entrance at the ceremony. I reminisced over how proud he's made me over the years. Now my beautiful son was getting ready to graduate college with a degree, I could not have been more proud as a mother. If only I could say the same for Martice sometimes – there was so much potential in him that he could not see in himself.

CHAPTER TWENTY-TWO

MARTICE

I decided that this Monday was going to be the Monday I would call off from work. Andre had the day off as well, so I figured I would spend the day with him. I picked him up and we went to Chicago Ridge Mall, then the Nike Outlet store on 87th Street on the southeast side. We ended our day with lunch at TGIFridays in Oak Lawn, a suburb near Chicago. Both my brother and mother were at work and they weren't expected to be home until about 5pm or so. I decided that Andre and I would go back to my house to chill for a while. I gave him a tour of our beautiful two-story house; I started in the living room and ended in the basement. I blushed when Andre said, "This house is as hell."

We sat in the living room watching the sixty-inch flat screen TV. As I turned on the TV it was planted on VH1 where the network was airing old episodes of Love and Hip Hop, so we decided to settle on that.

"I had a real nice time hanging out with you." Andre said as he was smiling and laying on the other couch opposite of me.

"I did, too. I'm glad I called off to hang out with you." I responded as I was taking a sip of my iced lemonade I poured for myself during the tour earlier.

"You all been living here a while?" He asked.

"Since 2005." I said.

"Cool!" was his response. He handed me his empty cup, and I quickly downed the last of the lemonade I had in mine. I washed out both cups and put them back up in the cabinet.

"Let's chill in my room for a second." I said to him as he jumped up and followed me upstairs. As soon as we entered into my room Andre kicked off his Jordan's and laid across my queen-sized bed.

"Don't fall asleep." I said to him smiling. He gave me the *yea, whatever, give me five minutes* look. I entered the bed and laid down beside him. Andre had his back toward me and I could smell his Burberry cologne and the weed he smoked earlier on him. I looked up at the ceiling thinking about how I said I was not going to get into a relationship anytime soon. It was amazing that here I was, damn near a month in, and I found me a new boo in Andre. Despite of what I heard about Andre we were taking things rather slowly, but were definitely moving forward. Everything was going as planned, and I had snagged the guy everybody wanted.

"Andre?" I said.

"Wassup?" He replied.

"How are you feeling about this, us, and what's going on? I just want to know because it crosses my mind from time to time. I know I don't usually have these types of conversations with you but..."

At that moment Andre interrupted me and turned over and kissed me - I kissed him back immediately. I felt my insides tingle a little and at that moment every question I had asked or anything that I did want to know did not matter. I pulled his shirt over his head and he did the same to me. I pushed him off me for a second and he gave me a *crazy, what's wrong* look.

"Let me cut the music on in case my brother comes home. He won't bother me if my music is playing." I said getting up and doing just that.

As I turned around from turning on the music in the bedroom Andre was fully naked. I excitedly ripped the rest of my clothes off, jump in the bed, an climb on top of him. Andre rolled me over and kept the kissing going. Although I was fully in the moment, I got slightly distracted. I thought about how I would be able to continue to keep this from my mother and brother. I was determined to make that be for as long as I could.

CHAPTER TWENTY-THREE

MARQUISE

"Quise, you ready to sing at the set on Saturday night, brotha?" David my co-worker asked me as we sat and ate lunch on break at work.

"Bro, as ready as I will ever be. You know I'm nervous but ain't nothin' that God can't see me through." I said eating shrimp-fried rice out the box from Rice Garden. This was the first time in months that I would not be singing Gospel music. There was an event my job was putting together and everyone put me up for singing for the event because they knew that I had vocals.

"Well you know Darrick was clowning you, saying you gonna do a sermon and shit..." David quickly caught himself. "I mean stuff, my bad, after you were done singing." David said laughing at his slip of the tongue.

I shook my head at David. Most times I got a lot of heat for being a pastor but it was a calling, and I was not ashamed of it.

"Bro, he needs a word." I said as me and David bumped fist.

"Man, I just want to thank you for introducing me to Powerhouse and Bishop Winston! He has that down south appeal." David said cheerfully.

"The Country Preacher is what they call him." I said and David agreed.

"And not even just that. I never liked going to church as a shorty. But at Powerhouse, with all the different things they have going on and the different things they have for my kids, I never want to miss a Sunday." David said.

I invited him to a service last April and two Sundays later him, his wife, Rachael, and their two daughters, Rayne and Riley were permanent members. I believe Bishop drew so many people because he was down to earth and his sermons were real. None of that pity-pat, let me give you what you want to hear preaching. Bishop Winston said what he meant, and meant everything that he would say. This is why I held the utmost respect for him. You either accepted the truth or you could resign from attending any and all services at Powerhouse Missionary Baptist Church.

"Bro, no problem! You know you have to have a covering for you, the wife, and kids. Powerhouse and Bishop Winston has been a beacon of light, not only to Parkersville, but the entire Chicagoland area." I said opening my can of Sprite and taking a sip.

"So how are you and Isis?" David asked.

"I'm gonna ask her to marry me at my grad party." I said as David stretched out his hand to give me a dab on the fist at the word of the good news.

"Congratulations, man! Man, that's one big step, you ready?" He said hopeful.

"As ready as I have always been. I'll be twenty-five, man, I feel it's time and I truly believe she is the one!" I said.

"Well, that's wassup, man. I gotta tell the wife when I get home, and we definitely will be making your grad party. And besides your uncle know he can que' some meat, dude!" He said swigging the rest of his Pepsi and throwing the can in the trash.

"Definitely, it will be plenty of food and there's going to be a DJ spinning. I even have a play area for the little kids.

There's going to be a volleyball net in the backyard, a horse shoe game going on, and cards." I said getting up looking at the clock on the wall realizing it was time to head back to our shift.

"Like I said, man, we not gonna miss it for the world. I'm happy for you, Quise. You really have did the damn, I mean, dang thing!!" He said laughing catching himself again.

"David, bro, you're good. We all fall short and it's not like you're irritating me with the cursing. Now, if you were, I would have to get my Bible out and read you a couple of scriptures. But you haven't gotten to that point where the Devil has taken over your mouth, yet." I said laughing with him as he was nudging me in the arm and laughing, too.

"All good, brother. Well let me get back to my side of the building, I'll chop it up with you later, Quise. And bro, I know you gonna kill the set on Saturday with whatever you choose to sing." David said walking the opposite way as we both exited the cafeteria area.

"Yea, I got the perfect song to sing on Saturday!" I yelled out to him in the distance between the two of us.

I picked the right song to sing for the night and couldn't wait to sing it; it was also one of Isis's favorite songs. Even after the incident at Westyn of not getting the apartment, which I had sort of gotten over, I knew God had something better in store for me. I just knew I had to be patient and wait on the blessing of the Lord.

As I was thinking to myself my phone vibrated in my pocket, I took it out of my pocket and looked at the screen. Isis had sent a text with the emoji of a smiley, kissy face with the words, "Love you, Baby", typed next to it. I smiled and typed, "Love you more!" I put the phone back in my pocket and walked back to my side of the plant to finish my shift.

CHAPTER TWENTY-FOUR

MARILYN

Finally getting home from work to enjoy my lunch break, I pulled into my garage and then let the garage door down. I decided to go through the back because I knew I would be home for a while. I got out of the car and walked around to the front of the house to see if there was any mail in the box. I was slightly surprised to see that Martice was already home. I made a face because I knew he normally worked on Mondays and I was wondering why he was home already.

I opened the mailbox and grabbed the letters out it, there was nothing in there but the normal bills - the gas bill, light bill, and a value shopper coupon pack. I looked at the mail and had a thought to go through it once I sat down at the kitchen table while I prepped dinner for the boys and me for tonight's meal before I went back to work. Coming through the back door, I cut the alarm off, and locked the door behind me. I went to my room taking off my jacket and laying it across the bed.

Being who I am I couldn't shake the wonder of why Martice was home. He wasn't sick the day before and I didn't know of any important business he needed to take care of, so it puzzled me of why he was home. I picked up the cordless phone in my room and checked the voicemail, there were no unheard messages. I put the phone back on the hook. I sat down on the bed and looked in my dresser mirror, but the sound of loud music and squeaking caught my attention.

I made a face and thought to myself, *now, why in the hell does he have that music blasting like that and why is there something squeaking in his room?* I was definitely about to surprise him by showing my face and finding out why he had the music so loud. And I couldn't help but wonder what the squeaking noise was. To me it sounded like his damn bed. I walked towards the steps and started walking up. At first I was going to just burst into his room until the sound of moaning coming from the room stopped me in my tracks.

I couldn't believe it, it was the moaning of sex with another male's voice saying sexual phrases. I walked slowly toward Martice's room hoping that I was imagining what I thought I was hearing, but the moaning got louder while running in rhythm with the bed squeaks. I was glad I took off my heels and my footsteps were rather light, it was impossible to hear anyone in the upstairs hallway if they didn't have shoes on.

I slowly brought my head to Martice's door, put my hand on the doorknob and tenderly turned the knob to open the door. As I peeked into the room my mouth dropped and I felt the insides of my stomach turning. I put my left hand over my mouth, as I could not believe what the hell I was seeing going on in my own damn house. I backed away from Martice's door as quietly as I could and closed the door. I dashed down the hall, back down the stairs, and into the bathroom by the kitchen where I vomited in the toilet.

I took the small blue towel I had hanging with another big towel from the towel bar, wet it with cold water and rubbed it all over my face, accidently taking off my makeup, in an attempt to cool my body down. I quietly put the towel up, put on my jacket as I nervously shook, grabbed my purse and keys, turned on the alarm, and made it out the back door to the garage. I got in my car turning it on while letting the garage door up, then down as I sped off back to Blue Cross Blue Shield. After what I had just seen, I could not stomach making any type of food right now at this point.

CHAPTER TWENTY-FIVE

MARTICE

Here it was a week later, things were definitely on the up-and-up with my relationship with Andre. After finally crossing the bridge of sex the prior Monday I called off, now I felt like I was officially his boyfriend. I got the chance to finally see his place in Englewood, and although I had no business hanging out in that part of the city, this was where Andre lived so I had to get use to going over there. He had a very nice apartment, it had bachelor's pad written all over it. That following weekend I hung out over there, he ordered pizza and we watched movies and just laid up and talked. This was what I had longed for after being off the dating train for a while. But at home something else was going on, my mother was very distant toward me the last few days. She did not say much to me, and I even caught her turning her nose up and giving me vile looks from time to time. I did not know whether to ask her if something was wrong or be afraid. She has never been like this, so whatever it is I'm hoping it passes soon, and very soon.

Once I got off work, I stopped at KFC and brought a bucket of grilled chicken with two sides of mash potatoes and some biscuits. I knew my mother would be making one of her famous salads, so I decided to get the potatoes as the other sides to go with it. Once Marquise came in, we all sat down at the table to eat and talk.

My mother started staring at me with the vile look again, and now I was feeling very uncomfortable. Every two seconds she would pick up her wine glass, drink, and then continue to stare. I just kept eating the food on my plate but also noticing the way she kept right on staring at me. Marquise was the first to break the silence in the kitchen with conversation.

"So anything new?" He asked the both of us.

"Nothin' on my end." I said quickly. My mother made a noise, looked at me again, and then started eating the food on her plate.

"Well, I got the tickets for graduation." Marquise said.

"How many did you get, baby?" Our mother asked him.

"There are a total of ten." He said drinking from his cup. I could not believe my brother was graduating from college, I was so happy for him. Now that he was about to take the extra step and move out, I definitely had to get on my shit and do the exact same.

"Well that's just about the right amount for the family and Isis." He said.

I got up from the table after finishing my food, threw away my garbage, and I decided to get ready to go to the mall with Treyshawn.

"I'm going to the mall, I'll be back later." I said.

"A'ight, bro, check you later." Marquise said.

I said "cool" to him and looked at my mother. She looked at me and rolled her eyes. I walked out the door and got into my car. I sat for a second thinking to myself, *whatever is going on with my mother, it has to be really deep because this attitude that she was giving me I don't know where it's coming from.* But one thing was for sure, I was getting tired of it and I was not going to kiss her ass to find out what her problem was now.

CHAPTER TWENTY-SIX

MARQUISE

I took Isis out to Red's on Saturday, it was a quaint neo-soul club that I used to perform at a few years ago before I became a minister. Even though I did not sing anymore I still would come and patronize the club from time to time. Ray, the owner, was like an uncle to me. I've known him since I was seventeen years old. I started out singing at Red's with a group that I sung with in high school. After the group parted ways I was doing solo shows there; singing old school songs on chosen nights. Red's was a very laid back spot and sometimes my mother would come here as well. There was no drama, the crowd was not young, and the soul food was always on point. Isis and I were seated at a booth and the waitress came over and took our orders promptly as we were seated. I was greeted by Ray as soon as he spotted the table we were seated at.

"Marquise, little brotha, so glad to see you!!" Ray said. I stood and gave him a man hug once he arrived at the booth. It had been almost a year since I had been in Red's. Ray turned and greeted Isis and they hugged as well.

"You gonna give us a song tonight?" Ray asked me.

"Ray, I really didn't come to sing." I said giving him a half crazy look.

"Just something quick. The people in here wanna hear you sing, man!" Ray said.

I looked at Isis and she smiled at me. "Well you got about twenty-minutes before the food arrives." she said.

I told Ray "cool", as he patted me on the back and dashed to the DJ booth to let him know I would be coming up to do a song.

"Well Red's, let's give it up for Marquise Johnson!" The DJ announced as the crowd of patrons gave me a round of applause. I made my way to the stage, talked with the piano player on the song I would be singing, and then positioned myself in front of the stage.

"Good evening, everybody! It's good to be at Red's tonight. I was asked to sing so I'm gonna keep it simple and

148

brief and do this little number for you." I said as I positioned myself in front of the microphone and the music to Musiq Soulchild's "Don't Change" started playing. I took a brief twenty seconds and then I started singing.

The entire time my focus was on Isis. She shyly smiled and dropped her head as I sung to her and smiled back. If I wasn't waiting the two weeks until the graduation party, tonight would have been the right and special moment to propose to Isis. But I wanted to share my special moment with my friends and family. I finished my song and thanked the crowd as I began to step down from the stage. They all stood up and clapped for me, including Isis.

I was on an emotional high from singing and the thought that Isis would soon be my fiancé. "God blessed me with you." I said to her as I returned back to our table.

Isis smiled, looked at me and said, "Yes, he sure did."

CHAPTER TWENTY-SEVEN

MARILYN

It was Saturday evening and I sat on the love seat facing the front door in the living room waiting on Martice to bring his ass in the house. Since the day I came home and caught him in bed with his co-worker I hadn't said as much as three words to him. I tried to block out the images, but at night they would awaken me out of my damn sleep. I didn't tell Marian or my mother about it, either. God knows what they both would have had to say. And no telling how Marquise would have taken it, as well.

I chose to keep it to myself, all the while I was furious on the inside and devastated. I did not raise my son to be a homosexual, nor was one going to live under my roof. Every day, since that dreadful day, I blasted Gospel music at 5 am in the morning as I was getting ready for work, which I knew irritated the hell out of Martice. I went around the house anointing everything with the holy oil I had gotten from Bishop Winston three Sundays ago. He'd given everyone in the congregation a bottle during service as a gift to take home and anoint our homes.

I even dabbed a significant amount in my hand and placed it on top of Martice's head while he was sleep. It scared the hell out of him as he jumped up and yelled, "What was the matter with me?" when I touched him. I just kept walking and quoting Bible scriptures anointing everything in the house. As much as the Bible taught against it, he still chooses to walk in rebellion and practice that nasty sin.

I had my suspicions about Martice and his sexuality but did not want to make any assumptions. I believe part of me wanted to be in denial about how my son lived his life. Even after seeing him in bed with his co-worker, I still held on to the hope that it was just something that I had imagined. I really wanted it to not be true, but whenever I saw that damn black Charger pull up and Martice would get out the passenger side, I knew that it was reality. That Monday continues to play in my head and I become angry instantly every time.

Like I said, I did not raise no faggots. That lifestyle is wrong and I was not going to stand for it. I had decided to implement a new curfew, and if he, so much as, got out of line about the new curfew, tonight was the night that I was going to put his ass out. I believed that giving him a curfew would keep him from seeing his co-worker. And also hanging out with that other boy that he calls a friend, who I know has got to be gay, too.

Rick was probably turning over in his grave right now, or even pointing a finger and laughing at me. I shook my head and lit another Virginia Slim. I had stopped smoking a year ago, but this shit that just happened made me go into a relapsed. So here I was sitting in this dark living room and lighting up the habit that was so hard for me to break in the first place. I was nervous and really didn't know what I was going to say to him when he walked through the door. I looked at the time on the clock on the wall - it said 2:59 am.

I heard a car pull up and a few seconds later I could hear the car door slammed. There was laughter and then footsteps coming up to the front door. Soon as the key went into the lock and it turned, like clock-work, I hit the lamp switch to turn on the light. As Martice opened the door his mouth dropped, he looked as if he wanted to piss in his pants when his eyes met mine. I was staring at him with no expression on my face at all.

152

"There are some changes that are going to take place as of right now." I said with an aggressive tone. He locked both doors behind him and put his keys back into his pocket.

"So you waited up for me to tell me this?" He asked looking at me.

"Don't try me, okay! Like I said, there are changes taking place in this house as of right now!" Getting up from the couch I walked over to get directly in his face. "Number one, you will come in this house no later than 1 am! Number two, I don't want to see that black Charger around here picking you up anymore. The neighbors have been complaining about a suspicious black Charger and it's drawing the wrong attention. Me and your daddy worked hard to get a house over here in the Evergreen Park neighborhood. I refuse to have some drama started and then they want us out."

I was just about to get to third rule when all of a sudden Martice yelled. "What?" He said in an angrily tone.

"You heard what I said! That Charger better not come around here any damn more!" I yelled back.

I did not know who he thought he was talking to but he had lost his last damn mind by yelling at me.

"And watch your tone when you talk to me. I don't know who you think you were just yelling at!" I said putting

153

my hands on my hips. Martice just looked at me before speaking.

"Who said that it's a problem with Andre coming by to get me?" He said with a little bit of his sass peeking through his anger.

"That does not matter, him or that car better not come back over here again!" I said walking away from him.

"I don't see what the problem is. So I don't see a reason as to why I should have to tell him that he cannot come by anymore or pick me up." Martice responded.

I turned around and looked at him like he really had lost his damn mind. At that point I could see that he had feelings for this boy by the way he was defending him. This caused my distain for the entire situation to come forth and I exploded.

"Well if you can't abide by the rules of this house, you can get your shit and get out!" I said to him pointing my index finger in his face. I was in thirty-six hours of labor with this boy, and I don't know who he thought he was talking to, but I was about to slap the shit out of him so he could remember.

"That's not a problem!" He yelled.

"Well get your shit and get out right now!" I yelled back blinking at him. Marquise came flying down the steps stepping in between the middle of us as he heard the commotion.

"What's going on down here?" He asked looking between the both of us. Neither me nor Martice paid attention to Marquise standing in between us, we kept our focuses on each other.

"Like I said, if you cannot handle the way I run my house you can get your shit and get the hell out!" Martice took one last look at me and then walked up the steps. Marquise looked to the steps then back at me with a puzzled look on his face. I looked at him and walked back through the kitchen to my room and slammed my bedroom door.

CHAPTER TWENTY-EIGHT

MARTICE

My mother said nothing but a word, Sunday while she was at church I grabbed most of my stuff and went to Andre's. I explained the situation to him and he told me that I could stay as long as I wanted. He went on to admit that he did not like getting up out of his sleep to take me home anyway when I should have just been right there with him anyway.

I spoke with Treyshawn the next day about what had transpired after he dropped me off at the house from hanging out at Hydrate with him. I was sitting in Andre's living room on the couch; Andre had left to go hang with some of his friends.

"Well, chile, you finally out! But moving in with Andre, I don't know, Tice!" Treyshawn said with uneasiness in his voice.

"What you mean, chile?" I asked him.

"Well y'all relationship is fresh, honey. It would have been better if you would have came and move in with me for a minute until you knew what your next move was gonna be." He said.

I was hearing him, but I wasn't. Although Treyshawn and I were good friend, I did not want to be staying with him and then our relationship takes a turn for the worse. I felt like staying with Andre was the better choice, especially since we were already in a relationship and it seemed to be progressing. Pictures of us together, smiling and doing different things were on his Facebook, Twitter, and Instagram pages - everyone knew that he and I were involved, now.

"Yea, but when you in love that's the only person you want to be around on an everyday basis." I said picking up the remote and turning on the fifty-six inch flat screen TV.

"Chile, whatever, you know that gets burned out really quick. Plus y'all just started heavily seeing each other. Know

that my door is always open if you change your mind."
Treyshawn said.

I was listening to him but it just was not sinking in. I
couldn't help it, I was on cloud nine and did not want to come
off. I looked forward to waking up to Andre every morning
and seeing his face before I went to bed.

"Well it's good to know that I can come and stay with
you just in case I needed to." I said smiling.

Treyshawn was truly a good friend and it was very
hard to find a good friend, especially when it came to gay
men. Most would not have your back, let alone tell you that
you could stay with them if they had their own place. Yet
they called themselves your "sis", "friend", "good Judy", and
all the other gay slang terms. This was why Treyshawn was
the only other gay guy I called a friend, not to put us down,
but when you see so much bullshit in the lifestyle it just
makes you sick at times.

"Yep, well chile, I got some things to do in a minute.
Let me talk to you a little later, okay?" Treyshawn said.

"Cool, call me later." I responded. He said "bye" and
hung up the phone.

I looked around the apartment; it was two bedrooms
with a small living room. The master bedroom had double
doors that you could access from the living room. His

bathroom was close to a door that you would go out of to go into the hallway. The building was a three-story with about eleven units - Andre's apartment was on the top floor. The Englewood neighborhood was saturated by poverty stricken households, full of gang activity, and drug infested. My hope was that maybe me and Andre could both move into a place out of this neighborhood in the near future. I sometimes dreamt and thought on how the future would be for us. My nose was very open to Andre. He was the only other thing that I cared about besides work and God, even though I did not attend church regularly.

Marquise texted me and asked, "Did you really get your things and leave today?"

I responded to the text and told him yes and that I would be back to get the remaining items within a week. His graduation and party were in two weeks and I planned on having all my stuff out of my mother's house before then. I wanted to avoid my mother as much as I could, but unfortunately I knew the next Sunday I have to attend church. Powerhouse was giving Marquise an award for being youth pastor for the last four years and celebrating that that he was graduating and getting his bachelor's degree.

At this point I did not have much to say to my mother, either, and didn't care about if we would regain a relationship. Marquise mentioned that she made comment and asked him if I had really left, I told him to tell her with bells on.

CHAPTER TWENTY-NINE

MARQUISE

I was traveling with my mother on the following Thursday evening to the Oakbrook Mall, a mall that was in the western suburbs of Chicago. We were going to look at a few suits and shoes to wear to church Sunday for when I received my award and the following weekend for graduation.

"You excited? These next two weekends are very important for you." My mother said while she was driving and I sat on the passenger side.

"Yeah, pretty much, it seems like it took forever to finally get this degree." I said.

"Yeah, baby, but look at all you have accomplished getting to this point. You have achieved a lot and I, for one, am definitely proud of you!" My mother said smiling at me.

I really wanted to ask her about the fight she and Martice had. Since he moved out with his friend it has been quieter than usual on certain days and nights. It was weird to me that my mother hasn't, so much as, asked if I have talked to him or seen him. Whatever they had gotten into it about my mother was not letting me know the reason.

"Ma, have you and Martice talked since he moved out?" I asked looking at her as she drove.

"No, I have not talked to your brother since the night of the argument." She said.

"Ma, I don't know why you two got into it, but we're family and whatever this is I'm praying about it and asked God to restore us. There is no reason that Martice should have left the house." I said.

My mother shot me a very evil and stern look, then she spoke, "Your brother does not want to abide by the rules of my house, then he gets disrespectful and mouthy, he needs to be out."

I could not believe my mother was acting like this. She was not letting up on the decision that she had made, which made me even more curious to what was really going on.

"Ma, being a Christian you know having this attitude ain't right." I said.

"Well I have prayed to God and I have prayed for your brother to get on the right path that I have bestowed upon you two as children. He's an adult now and he can choose to make his own decisions out of my house." She said matter-of-factly.

I shook my head and I said a silent prayer in my head for God. I prayed that he would bring things back and to work on my mother's heart. True, my brother might not be in the church like he was when we were kids, but God still had his back in any situation.

As I was deep into my thought, my mother finally arrived at the mall and pulled into one of the parking spots. We got out of the car and walked towards the entrance doors. The first place I headed to was Macy's in search of my suits and shoes. I had even thought about maybe going to Express for Men if I was not feeling the selection they had at Macy's. I tried on about three suits, I decided upon a black suit with a matching pink salmon tie, with a pair of clean, black, old school Stacey Adams. I took out my phone and texted Isis to see what she was doing. She responded that she was "eating dinner with Bishop and First Lady." I told her I would "call as soon as I got home."

The next text was to Martice, I asked him how he was doing today and how were things with him. His response was that he was "okay, and that things were going great." I texted back and told him that I would see him at the church on Sunday, and that I loved him. His response was "Yep, and he loved me, too."

CHAPTER THIRTY

MARILYN

"So I heard that you put Martice out the house?" My mother asked me on the phone when I came in from the mall after looking for suits for Marquise.

"Yes, I did! Martice has become very disrespectful, mama, and I'm tired of it!" I said.

I could tell that she must have spoken to Martice because she fired back at me with, "He said you set a curfew for him and told him one of his friends could not come by the house anymore?"

"I sure did because this person has been raising suspicion with my neighbors, as well as me. So, yes, I sure did tell him they could not come by any damn more!" I said sitting down at the kitchen table with a bottle of apple juice and my bowl of assorted fruit I took out the refrigerator to snack on.

"Marilyn something just does not make sense with this and before you say something hear me out. Now from what Martice tells me, he comes in from the club and you're sitting up waiting on him, and then you just start riding his case?"

"I wasn't riding his case." I responded to her question.

"Well, what was it then?" She asks me.

"What I told him was that I am tired of him coming in at very late hours every Saturday night. Then that car and guy were not allowed around here anymore, and if he could not understand that he could get his stuff and leave." I said, not backing down.

"So was the guy blasting loud music?" My mother was not letting up. Because my mother knows me so well I could tell that she knew there was more to why I really put Martice's ass out. To keep the secret about Martice's sexual orientation I felt I had no other choice but to make up a lie.

"Well Estelle, next door, said that a couple times he has blasted music." I said.

"Humm… It just seems like it's more to this than what is being said. I'm not saying it is you that is not telling me what it is, or maybe Martice is leaving some stuff out?"

"What all did he tell you?" I quickly asked cutting her off.

"Mainly what you just told me, but it just seems like it is not the entire reason. But I just wanted to hear your side." She paused for a second. "So have you at least talked to him since he left?" She continued.

I adjusted the phone and replied, "No."

"Marilyn, I think you should call him. Do you even know where he is?" My mother asked.

"No." I replied again as I was getting up and putting the bowl of fruit back into the refrigerator.

"Marilyn, I don't know what to say about you!"

"Mama, please, okay. Martice is grown man!" I said while I was rolling my eyes.

"Well, he's in the Englewood neighborhood, near Aberdeen and 79th street." She said knowing that would get my attention.

My eyebrow did raise hearing her say that. Now out of all places he lands his ass over there on that side of town where he knows all the shootings and killings is definitely in that area.

"Well I see he's been keeping in contact with you." I say to my mother.

"Marilyn, I talks to Martice all the time. Something you need to be doing and maybe you would have not had to put him out so quickly."

Annoyed once again by my mother's five dollar comments, I ended the conversation by telling her I would see her in a week, and my other line had another call coming through.

CHAPTER THIRTY-ONE

MARTICE

The sound system in Powerhouse sounded like the club on a Saturday night. I always truly believed that church was the club for the saints. When it came to certain choir songs that would be sung that would get everyone in the congregation on their feet gave me the same feeling of how when the DJ in the club played the right song to pull everyone to the dance floor. It was that type of Sunday - people were standing and clapping, waving their hands at my mother and the choir, and yelling out certain choir members' names to sing, and telling Solomon to "go 'head, you better direct!"

I invited Treyshawn to come to service with me just so he could see how it was. His family wasn't brought up in church and he really never had a church experience like Powerhouse's.

"Chile, church goin' up like the club on a tuesssdayyyy!" He said and I laughed at him. He was really feeling it. "Do you know what song they singing?" He asked me.

"Rev. Isaac Douglass & The Savannah Mass Choir's 'You Should be a Witness'!" I said shouting over the loudness of the choir.

"Chile your mama and them sopranos are bad! They betta sing and throw they heads from side to side!!!" He said trying to talk over the speakers as the announcing clerk came and gave the weekly church announcements. She could not get through another word before she felt the spirit and started dancing in the pulpit.

I gave the organ player a side-eye as I heard the sound of the old 70's disco record, "Le' Spank" by Le Pamplemousse being mixed in with other Holy Ghost sounds. There were about five sopranos that started shouting instantly and my mother got up to fan and console one. Bishop Winston got up from his chair and slowly made his way to the organ player, pointed at him, and mouthed,

"Keep it holy in here!" He said laughing and went back to his seat.

Treyshawn stood up as one of the ladies sitting near the mother's side of the congregation danced out of her seat and into the aisle. The ushers came and grabbed her, trying to catch ahold of her and fan her, she was really going wild style like Tina Turner with her dance. They let her keep going for a few more minutes before they tried to catch and console her again. By this time there was not a person in there seat. The organist had got to the breakdown part of "Le' Spank" and even I had to get back up because now I was feeling that myself. I stood and bobbed my head to the beat of the music. Shouts then rang out from the alto section and all I could see was hair and arms flying back and forth, about five ushers rushed up to that section to assist and calm the spirit of those who were caught up in it.

"Chile, the ushers was about to have to come get me in a second." Treyshawn said.

I looked at him and gave him a, *Like, really??? Sit down,* look while shaking my head and laughing at him. After about another thirty minutes of shouting the announcing clerk managed to pull herself and her wig back together to finish the announcements. Bishop Winston called everyone for altar prayer that lasted for another thirty minutes, then my mother sung a slow song, after which Bishop Winston came to the podium to preach.

"Saints of God, I had a sermon for you all, but the Lord told me them boys are in here today."

Treyshawn and I immediately looked at each other, and then he asked me, "Chile, who is the boys he talkin' about?"

"I dunno!" I said looking just as puzzled. I scanned the choir stand to the soprano section and my mother and I both locked eyes on each other for a brief second, and then looked the other way.

"You know I preaches the unadulterated truth. I don't exchange the truth for a lie! And when you come walking up in Powerhouse as a man you better come in here acting like a man!" Bishop Winston yelled in the mic and then the congregation followed with "wells" and "preach, Bishop". Treyshawn continued looking at me still unsure of what was going on; but I knew exactly where this was about to go. "Homosexuality and lesbianism is a sin! No matter how you look at it! The Lord did not make it for a man to lie down with a man, or a woman to lie down with a woman!"

Claps and "go heads" started to ring out from the congregation, I looked at Treyshawn and his expression quickly changed. He went from smiling and laughing to

straight-faced like he had sucked a whole bowl of lemons.
"They come up in here, switchin' and carryin' on, hand all
twisted, and loud. What you walkin' around here actin like a
woman, fah? And I'm not leaving out the bull-daggers, studs,
and dykes comin' in here walkin' hard like man and nodding
your head. Wat you walkin' around like a man, fah?" Bishop
Winston continued on and some of the congregation started
to laugh and make their own comments.

Treyshawn folded his arms and stared straight at
Bishop Winston with his head leaned to the side like a
woman listening to a lying man that cheated on her the night
before. I just closed my eyes as I felt a headache come on,
but said a silent prayer that Treyshawn did not act a fool and
yell something out at Bishop Winston that would embarrass
the both of us, and get him escorted out of the service.

"Hard legs rubbin' up against each other in the bed,
and you can't produce no baby just wastin' sperm!" Bishop
paused for a second. "Yes, I said it wastin' sperm!!" Bishop
Winston yelled out feeling the need to repeat himself and
half the congregation was on their feet waving their hands in
the air. "It's a demon and the Lord said come out from
among them! Get your soul saved and right before you
knock on the Devil's door and he lets you into hell!"

I looked at my brother who nodded his head looking
toward Bishop Winston from his seat. Treyshawn still

remained in the same state, head tilted, arms folded, with his lips poked up like he had been sucking on lemons. As Bishop Winston continued to preach down on the homosexual and lesbian lifestyle, I slowly looked around the congregation as some people were laughing, while others were cheering and applauding. I definitely felt some type of way, but then Treyshawn quickly got up, grabbed his keys, and marched out of the sanctuary doors. I felt bad for him because I was used to the way the church speaks on our lifestyles, but I don't think Treyshawn understood how blunt the church can be at times.

"That's right! Get on outta here!" Bishop Winston said and the congregation continued to clap and make noise.

I guess the good thing was that Treyshawn drove and did not ride with me, then I would have had to walk out right behind him and take him home. I can imagine how embarrassed I would have been because people would have known we were together. The media ministry had already put the cameras on him when he walked out, and you could see him from the screen monitors on the walls.

I could just imagine what he was going to have to say when I called him later. My eyes and head turned right around and met the stare of my mother from the soprano section of the choir. I lowered my eyes at her with the look of disgust, while an evil grin spread across her face toward me.

JEFFERY ROSHELL

CHAPTER THIRTY-TWO

MARQUISE

I received my award for outstanding service in the ministry and special recognition for graduating with my Bachelors in Information Technology. I was happy to have my mother and brother with me to take a photo, but I could tell there was still tension between the two and it was definitely high. They did not even say hello to each other after service while we were taking the family photo. My brother gave me a quick hug and made his way out of the sanctuary after the cameraman took the photo. I didn't even get a chance to ask him if he wanted to go to dinner with us, but I knew he would have said no. I just kept praying and praying that whatever the Devil was trying to do to my family

176

that he would loose and let it go. Isis and I took a few selfies together which I posted to my Facebook and IG pages. I was happy to have her join my mother and I at Gibson's in Oakbrook for my celebration dinner, my mom also invited my aunt Marian and her family.

As we set down to eat dinner my aunt didn't waste time asking where Martice was. My mother nonchalantly told her that she did not know and started talking about something at her job. My aunt tried to act like she didn't notice that my mother changed the subject, but you could tell she was concerned about why Martice wasn't there. My grandmother called me during dinner to see how I was doing and how everything was going. I told her the events that had taken place and she told me to pray to the Lord that he fixes the issues that are bothering my brother and mother. I asked her did she have any idea what was going on, and her response was no, but whatever it was my mother was not telling the entire truth.

After dinner and dropping Isis off at home, I called my brother and asked if I could come by where he was. He happily told me that I could. He gave me the address and I drove over. I pulled up to an apartment complex that appeared to be in a run-down drug infested area. There were several guys standing outside the building, more than likely pushing drugs, and they kept eyeing me inside while I sat in my Camry. I assumed they were watching so hard because they had never seen me or my car around the area before. Because I knew the area could be a little sketchy, I brought my .357 Magnum with me along with my gun card and had it in my glove compartment. Martice had a .38 Caliber as well, I wonder if he took it with him or if it was still at the house with the rest of his stuff that he left. My mom also had a gun, too. The three of us getting guns were her idea. She was concerned about all the crime in the city, and she wanted us to, not only have the blood of Jesus over us as a covering, but also a gun just in case.

I called Martice and let him know that I was outside of his building. He told me that was he on his way down the stairs and that we could go somewhere and talk. As I sat in the car waiting for him I noticed how the temperature was a pleasant 80 degrees on this Sunday evening in May. It made for a calming atmosphere to talk about something not so pleasant. My mother was looking for Martice to return his set of house keys back to her. And I had the uncomfortable task of being the middle man and asking when he was going to hand them over. I saw Martice come out of the gate that surrounded the complex and around to the passenger side of my car, where he opened the door and got in.

We both said "wassup" and pulled off from in front of the building. I figured we would ride to the park by the house which was quiet right now and it had not closed. It was a great place we could sit and talk for a second. As I parked the car we both got out and made our way to the park bench, with him on one side and me on the other.

"You hungry?" Were my first words to him.

"No, I ate before you came." He responded.

"Tice, wassup with you and mama, dude? I don't like this, you don't need to be out on your own in this neighborhood. And who is this dude you are living with?" I asked him all in one breath.

"Bro, I hear everything you saying, but I'm good. I won't be in this area for long but I had to get away from mama. I can't live with someone who rides me for nothing." He said.

I could feel the hurt in his words and I was concerned for my little brother. I grabbed his hand and told him let's pray. I said a ten minute prayer and pleaded with the Lord to watch over my brother while he was living where he was.

"Just as soon as I get approved for another apartment and move in, you're moving in with me!" I said looking at him.

"No, I'm okay, Quise. I don't need to move with you."
He said shaking his head at me.

"So you think you are okay living in Englewood with
all the murders and robberies that take place in that area?" I
said giving him the *you have got to be kidding me, you know
you're not safe* look.

"You're not safe anywhere in Chicago. Isn't this the
reason that ma took us to the gun range and we got the
cards and guns? It's happening in every community here."
He said which I could not disagree with him.

"I just want you to be careful, I am definitely worried
about you over here." I said.

"I know, but I'm telling you I will not be here that long.
Within a month or so I will be in a better spot." He said giving
me the stop worrying look.

"Why don't you just make up with ma and ask her can
you come back? I would rather you be back at the house, it's
only been a week."

"And give her the satisfaction that she won?! No,
Quise I'm not. All she will do is throw it up in my face that
she knew I could not stay gone without needing her. I am
going to do what I need to do so that she will see that I don't
need her for anything at all." He said.

I was, in a way, proud that my little brother had taken a stance to stand up for himself. My mother's problem was that she enabled me and my brother so much. It was an empowering feeling to know that now we both were showing her differently. We were showing her that we were coming into being men, and it was time for us to make our own life decisions.

"She asked me when you were going to give her your keys." I said to him.

"I have a surprise at the barbeque after my graduation on next Saturday." I said changing up the mood.

"What is it?" Martice said.

"Just wait, it's gonna shock everyone, but it's a good surprise." I said smiling, thinking to myself about the ring that I was going to give Isis. But more importantly how I had to get her finger size measurement without giving it away, I was a clever dude if I had to say so myself.

"Well good I can't wait to see granny, she even told me to pack up and come to Cali with her and get the hell out of Chicago." He said as we both started walking towards my car.

"Well, have you thought about that being an option?" I asked.

"Right now, no, I love Chicago. I'm not really ready to relocate and leave." He said getting into the car.

We talked until I pulled up in front of the building where he was staying again. He told me to text him and let him know that I made to the house. I told him I would.

During my drive home I listened to Elder Eric Thomas of The Greater Harvest Missionary Baptist Church, it was their Sunday evening broadcast and he was preaching. I felt the tears fall as I drove, I was worried about my little brother.

"Protect him, Father, and let nothing happen to my brother. Satan is busy and only you can restore and heal." I cried out loud.

As I was in my emotions I heard Elder Thomas prophesy, "What the Devil meant for your good! God is going to restore and put you back together, you just hold on! Change is gonna come!" As he ended his sermon, I was turning onto my block pulling up in front of my house.

CHAPTER THIRTY-THREE

MARILYN

I called the caterers and the bakery to make sure that the food and cake would be ready for Saturday afternoon. Then I called Ilene, over at the beauty shop, to confirm my hair and nail appointment for Friday night when I got off work. Lastly, I dialed Marian to make sure mama was okay for coming in off her flight from LAX on Thursday afternoon. I sighed at how there was so much to do in the next five days, if I could clone myself I would right about now.

I looked at the picture of me, Rick, and the boys when Marquise was six and Martice was four. I remember the day we took that picture like it was yesterday, we all looked so happy in that picture. It was such a shame things were so different. The memory of the animosity that I felt from Martice when his eyes met mine after Sunday service last week pierced my soul. If looks could kill, I would have been a prime target for him. After service he didn't utter as much as one word to me, and the feeling was mutual. I had nothing to say to his ass either. I forgot to ask him to give me the keys to the house, but Marquise told me that he spoke to Martice about it. I was happy to know that he would bring the keys by sometime this week coming up. I thought about where he was living, but quickly let the feeling go.

What an embarrassment to this family to be a homosexual, especially for me and his brother if the church were to know. I still had not discussed any of this with my mother, sister, or Marquise. Shoot, I'm still coping with the flashbacks I'm having from what I saw when I peeked through the door of his room. The images were frightening and engrained in my mind like a saw a dead body in a casket from a funeral. Every now and then I still felt the need to vomit just thinking about it. I sometimes think about where I went wrong as a parent? Who wants a faggot or a lesbian for a child? Or was someone touching him as a kid? All these things plagued my mind, but I was not about to accept it or condone it in my house. I stood on the true foundation of the word of Jesus Christ, God hates sin and that was a definite sin that I was not about to tolerate in my household under any circumstances.

I raised a man and not some fag, sissy, or wanna be woman who probably would be around here trying on my clothes and heels. Just the thought of him in my wigs, my stomach started to turn again. I tried to find out where he was living, but Marquise told me that he definitely did not want me knowing where he went.

I wished Martice didn't put me in this position, but I had a private investigator to locate him and I drove over there one afternoon. I decided to take an hour and a half lunch from work again and rode over to the address I was given by the private investigator. The area was definitely a place that I would not drop a dog off in, and the apartment complex was a three-story, scary looking building. I didn't dare get out of my car. I pulled up and glanced up to the top floor, where the apartment he was staying was supposedly. I shook my head, I could not understand why and how he would subject himself to this. Martice had a nice home and a lavish neighborhood to live in.

Some thugs saw me sitting in my car and came around the gate that enclosed the building to get a look inside my car and me. I quickly turned the ignition, put the car in reverse to get out of my parking spot, and then in drive and pulled off to the stoplight at the end of the corner.

CHAPTER THIRTY-FOUR

MARTICE

"Please enter your password." I dialed my password on my dial pad of my phone. "You have one new voicemail message, first message…" The automated voice said as I dialed into my voicemail.

"Chile, don't ever invite me to that church no more! And the only reason I did not get up and say somethin' is out of respect for you, your mama, and brother! Your pastor got the nerve to be callin' the kids out! And he got Passell Collins up in there on the usher board, passell the biggest Queen in Chicago! And had the nerve to be sittin' in the back wavin' his hand and clappin', and be at Club Escape every

Saturday night. Chile, boo! I'll call you back sometime this week!" Treyshawn said and the line went click.

"End of Message. To erase, press one. To save it press…" Before the automated voice continues to saying the next number I dialed one on my phone.

Treyshawn left the message last night, since the incident Sunday I had not heard from him but I kept calling him and calling him. I pretty much figured he was upset, but I was still a little embarrassed myself. It was Wednesday and I decided today would be a good day to go by the house and get some more of my stuff. My mother and brother both worked late and I did not want to run into neither of them, especially my mother. I knew that I was supposed to leave the keys, but I figured I'd just give her the keys on Saturday at Marquise's party.

I grabbed the mail out of the box, opened the door, and shut it locking it behind me. I went upstairs to my room and starting getting some more clothes and things and started putting them in bags. I bagged up all the things that I knew I could take with me. It took me about forty-five minutes to get all those things together that I was taking with me today. I made a dash down the steps into the kitchen. I grabbed a glass and put some ice and lemonade in it from out of the refrigerator and sat on the couch. My phone buzzed and caught me off guard, which caused me to spill the lemonade on one of the letters on the table.

"Damn!" I said to myself.

I picked the letter up and it was completely wet. I thought to myself I could just go and put everything back in the mailbox like I didn't get the mail. I didn't want to have to hear my mother's mouth about the mail, but she would still know that the letter had juice spilled on it. Either way she was going to have some shit to say, she would have known that I had been here. The first place she would have checked was my room to see who put the wet letter back in the box. She would have known it was me because she would have noticed that I had taken more items out of my room. I said, "Fuck it" and opened the letter to see what it said. It was from Chase Bank with my mother's name in the header as well as mine underneath it, I lowered my eyes as I read it...

Dear Mrs. Johnson:

It is time for you to upgrade The Children's Savings Account that you have for Martice Johnson to a regular savings account. We have a unique account we can offer you, that will give you best return on the ten-thousand that is currently being held.

Because Mr. Johnson is a legal adult, if you are unable to come in and convert the account, Mr. Johnson can do so himself by showing two forms of proper identification. Thank you so much for being a valued customer with us.

Sincerely,

Lisa Tomlinson

Personal Banker Chase Bank

I could not believe it! I had an account that my mother never disclosed to me with ten-thousand dollars in it for me. I looked at the letter one last time, then I folded it up and put it on the table. For about thirty seconds, I sat quietly and did not say a damn word. I didn't know whether or not to be happy or mad as hell. I kept wondering why my mother didn't tell me about this money. Whatever the reason was, all that seemed to invade my thoughts was that she knew and I was curious to know how long I had this amount of money waiting for me in the bank.

I got up, rinsed out the cup, and put it back in the cabinet. I went straight for my mother's room and I started, silently and carefully, going through her dresser drawers to find any evidence of the length of time I've had this secret account. Nothing is what I found. I went to the closet, opened it, and started going in suitcases and bags. *Damn, nothing but papers, clothes, and old pictures of my ancestors and her when she was younger.* I thought as I rummaged through the items. I found myself getting slight frustrated as it was nothing in here that was telling me what I wanted to know. I pushed everything back into place so that my mother would not know I was in her closet. She was good at knowing when things were not in place.

My foot accidently kicked against a small, red and black box. I bent down to the floor and opened it. I was curious as it had a picture of my daddy and my mother, me as a newborn baby, and Marquise. Marquise looked like he was about two, he was smiling with a head full of hair and had a pair of overalls on looking like a small, light-skinned version of the My Buddy doll. I smiled, and started going through other things in the box until I came to a four-part, folded letter in the box.

"It's from my daddy." I said to myself with curiosity. I opened it, and sat down on the edge of my mother's queen-sized bed and started to read…

Dear Marilyn,

I decided that before the last days of my life come to an end, while I am well enough, I should write this letter to you.

I owe you a letter of apology, and also words of advice for you as the future goes on. I wasn't the best husband for you, but you and the boys never went hungry or without anything. I sometimes wished I would have done things better, went to church with you and the boys, and also lived a life on the straight and narrow path. But that was not what I believe the Lord (as you always refer to him) had in store for me.

I cannot take back the things that I did - the gambling, and the women - but I will not let the fact that you came into this marriage with baggage yourself go unnoticed either! You are a damn good mother, don't get me wrong, and a very strong woman. That was one of the things that I admired about you, Marilyn. Even at such a young age you had it together more than most women that were me and your mother's age.

I believe that because of my age is the true reason that she did not want you to be with me. I was damn near her age at the time. But that still does not constitute for the fact that you have your own skeletons to deal with. I knew that closure and comfort for you was me adopting Marquise and giving him my last name, and making him my son.

I can imagine your shame of the fact that you could not deal with yourself, or the church knowing your secret. You were not even in college a good two years and you ended up getting pregnant because you thought his real daddy would eventually love you, leave his wife, and marry you like he promised. Now I'm not writing this letter to bash you in anyway, I have said it and I stick by it that I have felt very sorry for you. Like I said, you kept it together, birthed a child that a man was ashamed of, and did not want anything to do with you once he found out.

Damn shame what the outcome was when the First Lady of that church found out her husband, the pastor, was courting a younger woman behind her back while he was married to her. Lying to the both of you! Maybe that's why I never went to church, I just never trusted most ministers; I always believed that they were lying or hiding something. I know that it devastated you, and you kept quiet about the illegitimate child you found out you were carrying. I watched the man for years on television, preaching, and singing. He even sat in the pulpit back in the day with your own bishop. Have you told him any of this? Probably not I suspect. And I can understand why. That's how he met you while you were working for the church he was coming by and confiding in Reverend Winston (as you told it to me). I remember the story you told me of how he saw you working one day with the secretary of Powerhouse, sparked a conversation, and because of your love for yellow men with good looks, you were young and couldn't resist.

It's unfortunate that because you were young he played on you, lied to you, used you, and you got pregnant. Now I'm only repeating of what you have told me, this was all of a shock to me as well. I remember when the story made the news, "Pastor's Wife Has Him Murdered!!" Sent shocks throughout our whole community. She could not deal with it! With you! The affair! His lies! She paid a hit man to kill him, and now they both are buried side by side. She stroked out, probably due to her age as she was older than him. It probably was a mixture of all that she had to deal with in helping him start the church, and he was using her for her money, and getting big-headed because he was a famous young preacher on TV. But what I think what hurt her the most was that you were pregnant with his heir.

But even through all of that it did not stop me from loving you once we met. I loved you, married you, and then you gave me my own son, Martice Rick Johnson. That was the happiest moment in my life. I loved Marquise and loved that he was happy that I was the daddy that he thought he knew, but after having three girls, and then you have your own flesh and blood son, that was one of the happiest moments for us. Life for us had its ups and downs, but the one thing that you knew would tear the family apart, you have kept under wraps for years.

So I say my beloved wife, I applaud you. You are very clever woman. But have you thought that one day this all may come out? I know I swore an oath to never say anything, but it's hell trying to blocked this shit out of my mind. But as I am on my death bed getting ready to meet my maker soon, I just had to address this because in my eyes you need to tell Marquise the truth before you pass on!

Do not take this to your grave, Marilyn! You need closure and he needs to know the truth! I was not his real daddy! That jag-legged pastor was! And it's sad that his wife had to take that boy's daddy from him because of the indiscretions of you two!

I didn't write this letter to play tit for tat with what we both done in our past lives. But you know, as well as I do, that this definitely left you out of the running for best mother award. And the only way you will find peace is by telling the truth to Marquise before someone finds out and puts the shit out! Your mother and your sister are your protectors, but they have harmed the situation as well by hindering your ass! Yes, I said it! They have hindered your ass in this situation by keeping the secret which is more of a lie than a secret. Also, make sure that Martice gets the money I left him before he turns twenty-one. That's that boy's money! Don't you selfishly keep it until you feel he should get it. I know you. Your ass probably not even gonna let him know he has it! And that would be a shame for you to have spent so much time in the church and then you end up going to hell for the lies and bullshit you kept going while you were in church, playing with God but calling yourself a saved Christian woman.

You have to understand this is why I never went to church. Y'all Christians act like y'all so holy and keep up more shit than someone who don't go to church. Well, wife, I loved you, loved all my kids (including Marquise). Thank you for the years of marriage and giving me a son.

Rick

I closed the letter up. I felt my hand trembling and the blood running through my body boiling. I got up, put the letter back in the box, and put it back in the closet where I had gotten it from. I closed my mother's closet door, grabbed the bag of things I came to get, turned on the alarm system to leave. As I stood outside I put all the mail that I didn't open back in the box. I took the letter I had gotten from Chase, and stuffed it in my pocket. Put the bag with my stuff in it in the trunk of my car and drove away.

CHAPTER THIRTY-FIVE

MARQUISE

I was happy to be starting my vacation the Thursday of the week of my graduation and graduation party. I even started working on a few songs to sing at the party. Singing was my passion and I definitely wanted to get back to it, but I also loved ministering God's word to the people. I took Isis to lunch, we went to the place we had our first date, Carrabas. I ordered the spaghetti and she had the stuffed chicken breast with veggies.

"I am so proud of you, I can't stop smiling." She said looking at me.

I blushed a little as I looked at her admiring her beauty and the hot new hair cut she was adorning. Everything about Isis was great, she was that perfect five foot six height with a Coke bottle shape which I loved. "Baby, that hair style makes you look more mature and your beautiful skin is a nice compliment to it as well." I said smiling while trying to eat the salad that came before the main course.

"Babe, chew before you talk." She said then laughed.

"I was saying thank you!" I said chewing the last of my salad. The waitress made her way back to our table with some extra bread rolls and dipping oil. We both had peach ice teas to sip while we waited for our entrees to come. Our waitress Laura was giving us extraordinary service, she was definitely getting a tip today.

"Really, I had to catch you before you choked." She said laughing.

"Yeah, a'ight." I responded sipping the tea through the straw. Isis looked at me and smiled then she started to talk again.

"My granddad has found you a place! I overheard him talking to one of the deacons yesterday at home, but don't say anything, yet." She said.

I looked at her and smiled. I was trying to contain my excitement. I wasn't surprised that Bishop would be able to help me; he was well connected with a lot of people in the city. I believed wherever this place was I definitely was going to like it.

"I won't!! Thanks for giving me the heads up. After the discouragement with the Westyn Apartments I kinda stopped looking for a second." I said to her as the waitress sat our meals down in front of us and refilled our drinks.

"Yes, I know. When I didn't hear you talking any more about looking for an apartment I figured you were a little bummed. I mentioned it to granddad and he got right on top of it without hesitation." Isis said then taking a bit of her chicken breast.

That made me proud to hear that Bishop was looking out for me. I knew that marrying Isis was definitely going to be the best thing for me to do now. I now knew for sure that I had the backing of Bishop.

CHAPTER THIRTY-SIX

MARILYN

"I'm sorry, Mrs. Johnson, but Mr. Johnson came into the bank today and transferred the balance from that account to a private account. Unfortunately, I cannot give out that information." The bank teller had to repeat this to me three times on the phone before it finally sunk in. *How the hell did Martice find out about that money? And who told him?* I thought to myself.

"Thank you for your time." I said and hung up the phone quickly. I was sitting at my desk in my office and I started to feel a headache approaching. I was furious and definitely wanted answers. I picked up the phone and dialed Marian first.

"Hello." She answered hastily on the first ring.

"Now I'm only going to ask once and please do not lie to me because it was either you or mama! Who told Martice about that money?" I said matter-of-factly.

"I haven't said anything!" Marian replied quickly.

"See, I really don't want to have to go in on mama, but I know she gonna take me there if it was her that told him. I already told her that I would tell him when I was ready." I said to Marian.

I looked up to make sure my door was closed just in case a shouting match started to happen in the office. I was getting ready to call my mother and if she did, in fact, run her mouth somehow to that boy about that money she would be staying in Cali and not coming on Saturday. I knew the conversation we were going to have wasn't going to be nice, she was still my mother but she was about to hear some choice words from me.

"You really think mama did it, Marilyn?" Marian asked me.

"Hell, yeah!" I responded. I thought about how she kept saying that I needed to tell the boys because they were going to find out. If Marian didn't say anything there was no

203

other way for him to find out. I knew without a shadow of a doubt that she told him. No one else knew about it but me, Marian, mama, and Rick - and he took it to the grave with him.

"Alright, girl, let me call your mother and see what she has to say!" I said to Marian as I ended the call. I began preparing myself mentally for the call.

"Hello." My mother said so pleasantly.

"MAMA! WHO TOLD YOU TELL MARTICE ABOUT THE MONEY? WHY CAN'T YOU JUST LET ME DO SHIT BY MYSELF! DAMN!" I yelled.

"WHAT! WHAT ARE YOU TALKIN ABOUT, MARILYN???" She yelled back at me.

"Mama, you know damn well what I'm talking about! Don't act like you haven't said anything to Martice about the money Rick left him!" I said.

I know this was my mother but she had no right to go and say nothing about that money to Martice. I was his mother and I have the right to do things on my own terms. Her and I talked about this already, she knew I would tell him about that money when I felt he was ready to have that money.

"Marilyn! I have not told Martice about no money! I haven't spoken to Martice since he told me he was goin' by your house to get his shit!" She said.

I made a face, as her comment immediately caught my attention. "When was this?" I asked her.

"Yesterday." She said.

Then it made sense as to why his shoes were moved from by the back door. I had meant to check his room after noticing that. *Well, why didn't his ass leave his keys?* I thought. But how he found out about the money wasn't making sense to me.

"Well, if Marian and you didn't tell him who did?" I said.

The phone line had gotten quiet and out of nowhere my mother started laughing hysterically. "This is why I told your ass to tell them boys. You wait 'til now and guess what?? Your skeletons have come out the closet to expose you. It ain't no tellin' who told him but it wasn't me nor was it Marian." She said as it became eerily quiet again.

This really had me on the damn edge, I started to get a migraine. I looked in my desk drawer, took out my bottle of Aleve, popped two pills in my mouth, and drank some of my bottled water that I had.

"But let me say this. I hope whoever told him, you find out and before Saturday. I don't want to come home to some shit exploding at this party. And if you ever, call my phone and talk to me like you just did again, I will get on the first plane flying one-way to Chicago, and kick yo' ass!" She spat over the phone.

"Mama, I got to go!" I said through clenched teeth.

"BYEEEEEE!" She yelled back.

I hit the button quickly ending her call to call Marquise. "Hello." He said answering swiftly.

"Where's your brother." I asked him with an attitude.

"I haven't talked to him since Sunday when I saw him." He said.

"Hold on." I said putting him on hold and dialing Martice's number from my phone. It went straight to voicemail after the second ring, he screened my call.

"SHIT!" I said aloud.

"Mama, what's wrong and what's going on? Please can y'all just let Saturday pass and then after my graduation party y'all can act a fool. The church, Bishop, First Lady, Isis, and my friends will all be there. Please can you hold off on any arguments, let it go until after." Marquise pleaded.

I was listening to Marquise, but the way I felt, I could not promise him I would not act a fool on Saturday. "I will try!" I responded.

I then picked up my cell phone sending Martice a text to call me, which I knew the odds of me getting a response back was slim. He knew I knew about the money and now he was being spiteful.

"Mama, I don't need you to try, I need for you to do that, please!" Marquise said.

"Okay!" I said quickly only so he could let it go from bugging me about it.

"Why are you looking for him?" Marquise asked.

I paused and then spoke, "Because he stole ten-thousand dollars out of my checking account." I didn't mean to lie it just came out.

"What!?" Marquise said.

"Yes, that's why I'm looking for him." I said trying to figure out how to keep the lie going.

"I'm gonna call him right quick…"

"No!!!" I said cutting him off before I was exposed. "I will handle it myself, Marquise. You just concentrate on Saturday!" I said quickly to diffuse his concern.

"Mama, are you okay?" Marquise asked.

I pulled the mirror out that I had in my drawer and sat it on my desk. I looked into it to make sure I was looking okay and put it back in the drawer. I hesitated for a brief second and said, "I will be!"

CHAPTER THIRTY-SEVEN

MARTICE

I knew my mother and brother were calling me about the money. I kept sending them both to voicemail I had plans of dealing with them at the party on Saturday. All I kept thinking was about poor Marquise, all this time my father was not his daddy - this was definitely going to tear him apart. But my mother was lying to the both of us and I had to let him know. I took the money and put it in a savings account, I was thinking of how I could use the money to stack up and get my life in a better position. I mentioned what happened to Andre and he said that was the best thing for me to do.

I asked him if he would consider getting a place for us somewhere a lot safer. I was happy when he told me he would. He also asked if I could let him hold five-thousand to do so. Without even thinking about it, I told him I was going to the bank Friday to take the money out for him.

I was becoming very excited, it seemed like Andre and I was moving closer and closer to really being our own little family. He said that he would immediately start looking at some places in Oak Lawn, Chicago Ridge, or Palos Hills – all quaint and chic suburban areas outside of Chicago. I knew this was all going to work out for me. The best thing my mother did was tell me to leave - even though she didn't officially put me out.

Marquise texted me and told me, before the money incident, that my mother said that if I was ready to abide by her rules I could come back. I called bullshit. I was glad that I was out, on my own, and doing things that were right for me as an adult. I could not be cramped up in her house any longer having to deal with her bipolar attitude. Things were coming along for me, now I was just waiting on Andre to take the money and find us a place - somewhere else besides here in the Englewood area. I was getting tired of hearing the shooting throughout the night, but it only made me cling closer to Andre in the bed which wasn't so bad. All I could think about was how soon we would be out of this apartment and in nicer, calmer area.

CHAPTER THIRTY-EIGHT

MARQUISE

"Marquise Randy Johnson." Dr. Jerrod Phillips called my name over the microphone as my family and friends all went crazy in the stands with applause and praise. I shook Dr. Phillips' hand as he handed me my Information Technology Degree in the other. I walked down the stage steps and had flipped my tassel as I took a picture for the graduation photographer. I was all smiles nothing was killing my vibe today. I held the degree up in the air so my family could take their pictures from where they were sitting in the audience. The graduation lasted about a good three hours; the speaker was late and then some graduates were as well. I was just glad that I had finally gotten my Bachelor's Degree and was finished with school. Once I caught up with everyone, I hugged my mother, grandmother, Isis, and Martice, who then took off and said he would see me at the house. It was hilarious he hugged everyone but my mother.

"Baby, smile for the camera!" My mother said as I took a picture with Isis. I could not wait to get to the house. I was ready to give my future fiancé her ring after dinner. Today was going to be a very special day, all around. I was nervous because I did not know what to expect, but I knew that she would say yes. It was just in my gut that she would.

"We need to be getting to the house, I'm starving, shit! What time is Bishop and Robyn coming by?" My grandmother asked.

"Mama, they said they would be there about 3pm. That's the time I told them graduation would be about over." My mother said gathering her purse and phone as we all started heading for the exit door.

"Good because I'ma need to open up them bag of Doritos on your refrigerator. You talkin' about starving…" My grandmother said again as if she was about to die. I just looked at her and laughed.

"Mama, the food will be there just as soon as we get there. Once you undress and get out of those clothes it will be time to eat, and everyone with be there." My mother said as we made it to the location of the parking lot where our cars were.

"I'll see you all at the house. I'm going to drop Isis off so she can change and come to the house, too." I said as me and Isis got in my car and I started it up, but I rolled my window down to continue to talk to mama before leaving.

"Okay, well we will see you at the house." My mother said.

"Okay!" I said to them as I sped off.

CHAPTER THIRTY-NINE

MARILYN

Franky Beverly and Mazes "While I'm Alone" blared out of the two big speakers in my back yard. I had hired a DJ and sat out a few appetizers while I waited for the catered food to get to the house. My mother, Marian, and I managed to make three pans of baked macaroni and cheese, three pans of Bushes Baked Beans, a big pot of collard greens, and three pans of potato salad. My mouth was watering as I looked at all the delicious food we'd prepared. All we needed was the meats, fried chicken, fish, shrimp, pork chops, and steaks from the caterer to go along with the Hawaiian rolls that I had set out. Of course there were plenty of cases of pop and bottled water to wash it down.

My mother put her a bottle of Pink Moscato in my deep freezer; she kept saying how she couldn't wait for Bishop to leave so she can crack it open and let her hair down. I chuckled at her slightly and then a euphoric joy came over me as I watched Marquise enjoying his day. He was laughing and slapping high fives with Marian's husband and a few of his friends while they sat at the table talking about who was going to win the playoffs in basketball. This was a very important day in my baby's life and I was so happy for him and the accomplishment that he had achieved.

After a while all the food was sat out and the people were truly enjoying themselves. They were eating good and basking in the joy of the celebrations of my phenomenal son. I was busying myself around the yard while I was looking on the festivities.

"Marilyn, bring that other chicken out the house, this one pan is almost gone." My mother yelled over the music as James Brown's "Funky Good Time" came on. She had everyone laughing as she started cutting a step.

I shook my head, walked up the stairs from the patio and into the house to do just that. I grabbed the pan off the stove, first making sure that the foil was on it tight enough before I carried out of the house. I opened the door, but stopped dead in my tracks. I couldn't believe it, Martice and

216

the boy in the black Charger were walking toward everyone from behind the garage. I started to see red! I couldn't believe this shit at all. He had all the balls in the world to show up with him at my house after I told him not to bring him around anymore.

I watched Martice walk up to people and give them hugs and making small talk before moving on to the next crowd of people. My mother asked him who his fine friend was and the guy gave my mother a hug and said, "Andre". My mother was looking Andre up and down hard. I had to admit myself for a faggot he was very attractive, but hell, most of them were. I watched as my mother practically molested him, feeling up his muscular arms. He was in a fitted t-shirt that showed off his upper body and his arms were full of tattoos. From the looks of him I'd guess that he was Puerto Rican and Black mixed – I was pretty confident because he had this certain hair texture and skin complexion that usually is a trait of men mixed with both cultures. I noticed that he had the dark eyes that were chilling, but made him appear even more attractive.

Martice had definitely brought the Devil to my house this afternoon, but I was ready. I know I had promised Marquise I wouldn't act a fool, but this shit right here in my face, I was definitely about to show my ass in front of everyone. Martice caught my express and smiled at me. I walked down the steps, placed the chicken on the table, and walked over to him.

"You got my keys?" I said and he and Andre looked at me. Martice handed me my keys. Andre spoke to me but I gave him a very cold look, he caught it and looked away from me immediately.

"Martice, baby, make you and your friend something to eat there's plenty of food." My mother yelled from across the yard.

"Naw, grandma, I just came to speak and get the rest of my things that are here." He said.

"Martice!" Marquise yelled as ran up and hugged his brother. "Bro, I need to talk to you about something." Marquise said as he let go and gave his attention back to the party. "Can I have everyone's attention?" Marquise bellowed out to the party as he grabbed the mic from the DJ.

"I wanna, first, say thanks to you all for coming. This means so much to me that everyone is sharing my special day of graduation with me. But this is only part of my special day!"

I saw Marquise grab a small bag from the DJ's table, he walked over to where Isis was sitting with Bishop and First Lady at the table. My heart dropped to floor as I saw him get on one knee, my mother started yelling, and Bishop and First Lady both stood up along with all the other guests who were in attendance. Isis started crying as Marquise opened the bag and took out a small black box from Rogers & Hollands' jewelry store. Kneeling on one knee, displaying the beautiful opened box with the large diamond engagement ring in it, he then sweetly asked Isis to marry him. She answered with a tearful "yes", and held out her hand as he placed the ring on her ring finger. They embraced each other and kissed.

"Glory be to the Father! Welcome to the family, son!" Bishop Winston said as everyone clapped.

I immediately ran up the stairs and into the house. I couldn't believe this; first moving out and now marriage!! He was not ready! What the hell was wrong with him? I heard my mother come in the house.

"Marilyn, what's wrong with you?" My mama said confused.

"Nothing, mama!!" I said with my back turned to her with my hands on my hips.

"Marilyn, you have got to let them boys go. They are grown. You are their hindrance, stop it!" She yelled at me.

"Mama, please don't tell me how to raise my kids or what I need to be doing with them." I said to her. Before she could cut into me Martice came into the house.

"Granny, I'm about to leave." He said to her looking at me with a smile.

"Baby, at least take you some food, okay." She said to him giving him a hug.

"Naw, I'm not hungry, but what a celebration this has turned out! Marquise getting married and I'm so happy for him!" Martice said looking at me and smiling, clearly trying to get under my skin.

"Don't patronize me in my house. If you came to get your shit, then get it and go!" I said heated.

"I think you should shut up talkin' to me while you are a head, Marilyn!" He said giving me a disgusted look, walking toward the back door. My mother, who was visibly shocked, and I both looked at each other and then jumped up, running behind him. We were hot on his damn heels.

"What did you just say to me?" I yelled at him as he pushed open the back door and I did the same not knowing if it slammed on my mother.

"You heard what I said, Marilyn!" He said being even more disdainful.

"Martice! Don't you talk to your mother like that!" My mother said as we had everyone's attention.

"Granny, please don't mention that word. What kind of mother has me and Marquise really had all these years? All the lies she's been telling, secrets she's been keeping. Don't tell me how to talk to a woman who has been lying to me and my brother for years!"

My mother's mouth dropped open. I started to breathe heavily; my mother was right, my skeletons had found the key to unlock themselves from out of the closet they had been in all these years and they were definitely ready to come out and play.

"What you talkin' about, Martice?" Marquise asked him as he was walking over to the two of us as we stood in front of each other in a stare off.

"Ask your mother!" Martice said with the Devil's grin on his face.

"Bro, I've been meaning to talk to you about the money that's missing from mama..." Marquise was beginning to say but he couldn't finish because Martice made a face and his eyes got bugged out of his head.

"That's my damn money! My damn money that she's been lying about that my father left for me." He then turned from looking at Marquise to my direction and continued yelling. "Something she's been too trifling to let me know about!" I could see the hurt over his face.

"Mama! I thought you said Martice took that money!" Marquise said. I was too paralyzed with shock to respond.

"That's just one of her many lies. You haven't heard the best one yet!" Martice said smiling.

Before he could say another word, I thought it would be best if I cut him off. "Well, since you airing out dirty laundry, faggot, don't forget about your own!" I heard the crowd gasp at the insinuating accusation. "That's right! Tell everyone how I caught you and your friend you brought up in here in the bed fucking! Listening to you moan like a ho!" I yelled at him getting up in his face. I heard different voices starting to whisper and even got a glimpse of some facial expressions.

"Hey, y'all take this in the house!" My mother said coming over to me and Martice.

"No, granny, she's right. I'd rather sound like a whore, than actually be one who was sleeping with a married pastor! Then try to conceal my pregnancy by him so the church wouldn't know and putting on a front. You ain't holy at all, Marilyn! That's right! Did you think that pastor was gonna leave his wife for you?? His whore on the side because you got pregnant! That's right! Tell Marquise who his daddy is!" Martice said.

I hauled off and slapped Martice so hard that his head flew back. My mother was physically staggered by what was happening and that she was struggling to get a handle on it. She yelled for us to stop it and to calm down. I was on fire

222

and furious! I could not believe the show that we were putting on in front of our family and some of the church members that were here. They were all getting a show that I'm sure they would never forget.

As I thought about what Martice was saying, it all made sense to how he found out. My head started spinning furiously, I now realized that Martice had read the letter that Rick wrote before he passed. I walked over to him as tears streamed down his face; I took my hand and grabbed his chin turning it towards me.

"Martice, I'll be in the car." Andre said from out of nowhere.

I looked at Andre as he looked at me but then he started walking to his car. He gave me a look with a sneaky smirk that I recognized all too well. I put my other hand up for my mother to calm down before she could say anything to Andre and I let her know I had this.

Giving my attention back to Martice I said, "So has he asked you for any of that money, yet? I bet you done gave him half! I grabbed martice's chin with my hand bringing his face to mine like a bad child in trouble, Let me tell you something, he ain't gonna do nothin' but get tired of your ass and put you out! And then where you gonna go? Cause you can't bring your ass back up in here! You get the rest of your shit and get the hell out of my house!"

Martice snatched away from me and walked toward the Charger, he got in and he and Andre took off down the alleyway. I turned my attention towards everyone, they all were speechless and I saw Marquise and his eyes met mine. I could see the disappointment written all over his face. I tried to speak, but he walked away from me. My mother looked at me, shook her head, and ran off to follow him with Isis right behind her. I looked at everyone again, Bishop Winston and First Lady started praying and so did some of the other church members. They joined each other in a circle while the other crowd of people, including Marian and her family, just continued to stare at me like *what's next*. I walked up the back steps to my back door, walked in and then to my room. I slammed my bedroom door behind me and didn't come out for the rest of the evening.

FIVE MONTHS LATER...

CHAPTER FORTY

MARTICE

I sat in Hydrate with Treyshawn on a blazing hot Saturday night in September. I decided to hang out with him since it had been a minute since we had done such. It has been five months since I have spoken with my mother. Ever since the incident, I had not heard a word from her nor had she heard anything from me. Marquise and I would text every now and then, but he did not want me to know where he was as of right now because he, too, was still not talking to our mother. My grandmother would call me every now and again, she would occasionally throw in a "have a talked with your mother" suggestion, to which I would always tell her no. I think my grandmother was concerned about us talking to our mother because her birthday was coming up on July tenth. Although I tried not to care, but I did wonder how she was going to be celebrating her forty-third birthday, especially since she did not have me or Marquise with her.

"Chile, it's kicked and dead. I'm gonna have one more drink and then we can go." Treyshawn said. I nodded okay at him and I ordered us two more blue motherfuckers cocktail drinks. "So, how are things with you and Andre?" He asked.

"It's okay. It feels like we've been together for years and not only five months". I said sipping my drink.

"Well good. I'm glad to hear that, chile. You seem really happy." Treyshawn said.

"And I am. I couldn't ask for a better boyfriend." I said holding up the drink.

"Chile, I'm still in shocked at you and your family. All that shit that happened and your brother still ain't talked to your mother? It's been five months she has got to be out of her mind?" Treyshawn said with concern in his voice.

I gulped the rest of the drink down and threw the cup in the garbage. "Well, she's not budging and I know for a fact Marquise doesn't want shit to do with her. As far as I'm concerned, it was just the money thing I was mad about. I already know her real issue with me is that I'm gay."

"Chile, she will get over it! People swear up and down, just like the church folk that you were not born gay and it's a demon. Get the fuck out of here! Then explain this to me why do you have all those choir directors, men in the choir, and pastors that are gay? When you can explain that to me then I will reason with your view." Treyshawn said sipping the drink.

"I have always questioned that." I said.

"And there you go." Treyshawn tipped his head to me.

To understand why so many were gay in the church was something that baffled me for years. I even tried to ask God in a prayer why were there so many homosexuals in the church. If it was so wrong why couldn't he just take these feelings out of my body and make me straight. I eventually gave up these wishes and started accepting myself to a certain extent; however, I would continue to hide it because I was not ready to deal with it publically. But now that I was out it was the most liberating feeling that I could ever experience.

My granny was curious about when I knew I was gay. In our short conversations over the past months she probed into my whole gay lifestyle. She also asked why did I introduce Andre as my friend and not my boyfriend? I simply told her because everyone would not have understood; especially since I had not yet come out of the closet. Her response was, "fuck everybody's understanding" and for me to do me. This is one of the reasons why I loved my granny so much. I apologized to her for what I had done and she said she forgave me. But being granny, she also told me the person I definitely needed to give an apology to was my mother. I told her that would be when hell froze over. She knew my mother was not speaking to me and I the feeling was mutual. And being the Cancer woman that my mother was she knew she could hold a grudge for a long time.

"Chile, let's move!" Treyshawn said as we both got up and started walking to the exit.

Treyshawn dropped me off at home making sure I got inside the building first before he pulled off. I turned my key in the lock, opened the door and closed it, and locked it behind me. Andre still was not home and it was working on 4 am.

I couldn't believe it so I texted him. "Are you on your way home?" It took Andre fifteen minutes to respond back to me. That really got under my skin.

"No. Still out with my people. We went from one club to the next but we're still partying." He responded back.

I made a face at the comment. I sighed and sent out another text. "When are we gonna go look for a better place?" His response came in much quicker than from the first one.

"Bae, let's talk about that later. I'm out. See you whenever I come in."

"Whenever I come in." I said aloud reading the latter part of his text.

I grabbed my phone, walked to the bedroom, plugged the charger into the wall and put the port into the phone. I grabbed a pair of shorts and a shirt out of the drawer and put them on the bed. I would change into this after the hot shower I was getting ready to take. I could not believe he just told me whenever he comes in, that was a first. It's 4 am in the morning he should be on his way coming home not extending his night out. I got up and went to the bathroom to take my shower.

CHAPTER FORTY-ONE

MARQUISE

My phone began to ring, I picked up the phone to see who was calling, it was my grandmother's name flashing across the screen, and I answered it. "Hello." I said.

"Marquise, baby, it's grandma, can you talk?" She asked.

I put my earpiece in so I could hear her loud and clear. "Yeah, granny, I can talk." I said.

"Well how you been?" She asked.

"I've been fine, granny." I said. It had been about two months since I talked with my granny and five since I talked with my mother. I didn't know who my mother was anymore. I couldn't shake that she had been lying to me all these years having me to believe my father was Martice's father. I prayed and asked God for guidance and how to accept it. But no luck, I found myself almost hating my mother, which I knew was not good. I tried my best to act cordial in church, but when I would see her at church I couldn't help but to ignore her.

I eventually got the majority of my clothes out while she was at work. I knew when she discovered this she would be hurt, but right now I still had nothing to say to her. Bishop Winston would arrange meetings for us to talk, but I would always decline. I was just not ready to face my mother or the reality that my father was not the man I thought he was for all these years. I didn't know how my mother lived with herself holding in this secret for all these years. Seeing her at church she looked depressed and sad. She managed to keep it together, but there were a few times when certain songs were sung she would start crying and screaming, catching the spirit for consoling. She was really going through, but I was also having a hard time adjusting to the reality of the situation myself. It got quiet on the phone before my granny spoke again.

"Baby, you really need to talk to your mother and make amends with her."

"Granny, I'm not ready to talk to her, yet." I answered.

"And when do you think you're going to be ready, baby?" She continued to probe.

I didn't know what to say or how to say it. I was hurt and confused; I wanted answers on who my father was and why my mother lied to me about him in the first place. I just wanted things to go back to normal.

"I don't know, granny, maybe soon." I said to get her off my case about it.

"Well, baby, you make sure you do. At the end of the day that's still your mama, she may have made a very dumb ass mistake, but no matter what, baby, you cannot hate her."

I was listening to my grandmother and knew I had to do the Christian thing and have a conversation with my mother. I had sent her a one worded card for her birthday last month, but other than that I did not have much to say to her.

"Well I've been praying and I hope you and your brother can sit down with your mother and have a talk. Y'all need closure to this. It's been five months, and to me, that's far too long for this to still be going on." She said and then there was a pause. "Baby, that's my other line, let me call you back." She said quickly.

" Okay, granny." I said hanging up the line.

I was happy that Bishop Winston had provided a place for me to stay for the past few months which were an apartment that he owned, but he was soon going to be renting it out. The place that he had finally found for me was in Palos Hills and it was even better than the Westyn Apartments. When he finally told me about it, I had to act like I didn't already know about it. But as soon the cat was out of the bag, I jumped on it working with the leasing agent so I could get approved as soon as I possibly could.

I was so excited, everything was all set for me to move in the first of November. I made sure for the next two months to stay on top of my planning and preparing so that everything would be lined up perfectly. I was definitely ready to move and finally be on my own and start enjoying my independent life.

As I sat and thought about my own life, I couldn't help but think about what my mother could be doing right now. I know she missed me, and I missed her too, but then the thought of being betrayed with the lies would always play over and over in my mind. I just did not know what to do and I was asking God to show me the way out of this situation and the anger that I held on to.

CHAPTER FORTY-TWO

MARILYN

The last few days and months have been rough for me. The day of the altercation with Martice, I called Marquise about a thousand times and each time he sent me to voicemail. I was so hurt that he just did not want to talk to me. It still hurts that even months later he refuses to talk to me, even when he sees me in church on Sundays, I barely even got him to look my way – it was like I didn't exist to him. I was hurt, disgusted, and devastated that the entire thing played out the way it did. I prayed to God every night to forgive me for what I had done. There were nights I sat up and cried, and prayed, and cried some more. I was told to

236

leave it in God's hands, and that he would heal and restore my family.

My mother asked me had I talked with Martice since the incident. The truth was that a part of me was hurting because of the situation with him, but I was solely concerned with Marquise. I had to talk with Marquise and explain to him why I did what I did. I thought this was something that I would have been able to take to my grave and it just wasn't. I guess the Bible is right when it says what is done in the dark always comes to light. My mother always told me that keeping secrets only created dangerous avenues for them to come out. She never let me forget on how she's always told me that I should have just told Marquise when he was of age about his biological father.

I sat in the choir stand getting ready for service, it had just started, and it was now time for the choir to sing our first selection. I saw Solomon walk over to Marquise and whisper in his ear, Marquise got up and went and stood at the podium. I knew this meant that he was about to sing a solo, but for what song? Some of the Voices members that were in the congregation started to ring out with "Sing, Marquise, let the Lord use you." Solomon stood the choir up and the melody of Daryl Coley's "When Sunday Comes" started playing on the organ. As Marquise started singing the words, I could hear the emotion that he was putting into the song, and the congregants and the associate ministers in the pulpit started to stand on their feet as his voice moved with the melody.

"Jesus will soothe myyyyy trouble minddddddddddddddd! And all of my heart aches, every burden, all of my misery, every trial, every tribulation, will beeeeee left behinddddddddddd!" He belted out.

As he sung, I felt the tears roll down my face. One of the sopranos behind me must have saw me because I felt a fan going behind me making my hair flap back and forth and then she handed me tissue. Solomon raised his hands and the choir started to sing along with Marquise. He was really driving the song, he grabbed the mic from the mic stand and started walking from one side of the pulpit to the next. As he was singing the words, getting to the special, he got down on his knees with real emotion.

He drove the song as the choir kept repeating "Sunday" and he sung singing, "Everything, was going to be alright." The church was messed up, screams and shouts rang out, I could see some congregants crying themselves, I could not stop crying and I felt the power of God moving. As the song ended Marquise put the mic back on the podium hook. He slowly walked towards the soprano section and stopped and looked at me. It was at that moment I ran from around the first row and hugged my oldest son like he had just come home from the army. I cried, he cried, and the church continued to ring out with shouts, praises, and thank you Jesus' as everyone stood on their feet.

CHAPTER FORTY-THREE

MARTICE

The weekend rolled around rather quickly. I was sitting on the couch watching TV when Andre came in.

"Hey." I said to him.

"Sup." He replied back.

"Nothin', how was work?" I asked.

"It was decent." He said and then he looked at me and sat down beside me. "I got a question, well more like a favor to ask." He said.

I turned the TV down just a little to hear what he had to say and then directed my attention to him.

JEFFERY ROSHELL

"You think you could go stay at Treyshawn's in about two weeks for, maybe, the weekend? I got my cousin comin' in from out of town and he don't know that I get down." He said staring at me.

For a moment I held on to it, but then I simply replied, "No problem, I will ask him." I said.

"Cool! I don't need him all in my business, you know?"

"Bae, you already know, I got you." I said getting up and giving him a kiss.

"Cool, you ready for me to wear that out." He said patting me on the ass. I shook my head and smiled at him, but knew what was about to go down. As he was walking away he looked back at me and told me to meet him in the bedroom, and I did.

"Chile, of course you can come stay with me that weekend. We can chill, hang out, and talk shit!" Treyshawn said over the phone.

I had called him right after me and Andre finished having sex – Andre was in the bedroom sleeping. I needed to know as soon as possible, but I knew it wouldn't have been any issues. Treyshawn barely did anything in the summer and he didn't have company like that all the time.

"Well I just wanted to confirm it with you first." I said.

241

"And chile, you know it's all good!"

"Cool, cool!" I said as I heard the buzzer sound. I got up and walked up to the intercom and I asked who it was - it was FedEx with a package for Andre. He was always ordering something around the beginning of the month. I sat it on the table just like I would do the others that I got before he came in the house. I asked him what they were and he said things for his job.

"Chile, I thought you and Andre was moving once you gave him that money?" Treyshawn asked.

"It's still in the makings. We are still looking at a few other spots." I said looking out the window from the top floor.

"And what about the money, chile? So he's still holding on to that as well?" He said inquisitively.

"Yeah!" I said slightly irritated. *What's up with these twenty-one fucking questions?* I thought to myself. I then noticed that Treyshawn had gotten quiet. "Why you get so quiet?" I asked.

"Chile, is Andre around you?" Treyshawn asked.

"No." I responded.

"Tice, let me ask you something. Do you think giving him that money was the right thing?"

"Yea, it's just that right now we can't seem to find a place. You know vacancies are not really good in the summertime in Chicago, the winter is when most places have availability for apartments." I said, then it was another five second pause.

"Chile, you my good Judy, and listen to me when I tell you this. I'm not saying that you shouldn't have given him that money, and I'm not saying that he might have done something with it, but Martice please be careful. Make sure you're keeping your eyes and ears open to everything that is going on, including him, while you are with him at that apartment."

I made a face, what the fuck was Treyshawn talking about? He sounded just like my mother the day we got into it and she made that comment, "He ain't gonna do nothin', but get tired of your ass and put you out!" I remembered her saying. But I quickly dismissed that. If he was really going to put me out it would have happened by now. Why hadn't he put me out already and here it was going on five months.

I realized that the hate and shade was real, my mother needed a man, and Treyshawn out of all people, I couldn't believe he was coming for me like that. He probably was just as upset because he wasn't in a relationship right now. Sissies love to hate no matter what the situation, if another gay dude was doing better than them, they had to shade or talk shit. *Damn we really have the crabs in the barrel mentality, just be happy for me like the friend that you're supposed to be*, I was saying to myself in my head.

"I hear you, I ain't no fool." I said to him while rolling my eyes.

CHAPTER FORTY-FOUR

MARQUISE

I pulled up to the Washington Memorial Gardens Cemetery in Homewood. My mother had told me to meet her there, for what reason I did not know. As I was driving through the cemetery, I saw her Charger and parked right behind it. She got out and stood waiting for me to do the same. I hit the lock button and joined her walking toward some headstones. We walked up to a nice headstone that read "Beloved Pastor, Son, and Friend. Rev. Josiah B. Worthington 1965-1993."

"This is your real father." My mother spoke softly as we stood and gazed at the headstone. All I could do was look at it. I was frozen in a daze and could not come out of it, honestly, I did not know what to say, what to feel, or think right now.

"What happened to him?" I managed to finally finding the words to come out.

"His wife, the first lady of the church, had someone murder him when she found out about me. I was young and was under the impression that he was going to divorce her because things were not working out for them. Well he never left her, but he kept the affair going with me. I eventually told him I was done and could not see him anymore. I couldn't deal with him continuing to promise me that he was leaving her, but then I became pregnant with you.

"We found out that his wife had hired a private investigator and found out about me. It was not even a week later from her finding out that she had him killed. It was all over the news and the television, no one seemed to understand how this great pastor who came on television, always doing something in the community, and could preach God down from heaven, could have his life taken like that."

I continued to look at the headstone as my mother went on with the story. "All I could do was cry. I was so hurt, no one knew about the affair, but I had to tell someone so I told your grandmother. She was devastated finding out the truth of why he was killed. She knew he was rather comfortable talking and speaking to me whenever he came by Powerhouse, but she thought it was because I worked in the secretary's office at the time. Well, it finally surfaced who killed him and why when his wife confessed to it. She said she could not handle him messing around on her and he promised her that he would never break her heart. She stood trial, but eventually died while in custody of a literal broken heart they said."

I heard my mother start crying as she reminisced over the tragic events, I reached over and hugged her. She continued speaking, "I have never felt so ashamed of what I've done than I do now after all these years. I tried to conceal and hide it because I thought that was in the best interest of you. You don't know the day to day pain of knowing the truth but too afraid to tell it. I would just block it out, Marquise. I really did not know how to tell you, and I thought by just taking this to the grave with me it would never come out. But the reality of it, you were going to eventually find out about your real daddy and that Rick was not your father.

"I just did not want to accept that or hoped that when I passed on, if it came out that you would have forgiven me and understood why I did it. These past months of not knowing where you were or seeing you at church and you were not speaking to me has been hell. And I am sorry for not telling you any of this. I did not know how you would have reacted to it."

I was listening to my mother. I honestly heard the sincerity in her voice. She was crying her eyes out and I knew I could no longer hold the grudge against her. At this point I was able to empathize with her and see from her perspective. I had known about all that Martice's daddy had put her through, and to find out the things with my mother, I could now understand some things about her.

"Ma, I forgive you. I forgave you when it happened I just didn't know how to let go the hurt. I prayed to God to show me the way; how to let go of the hurt and pain of the things that I didn't understand. Well he did and I'm grateful for it." I said as I looked upon her grieving, yet relieved face. I gave her a hug and continued to tell her that I forgave her while she cried in my arms rocking back and forth saying, "Thank you, Jesus! I'm sorry, Lord! I'm so sorry, Lord! Thank you, Jeeeeesussssss!!!!" I felt the power of God moving, like he always moves, but at this moment he was here in the cemetery with us to set us free!!

CHAPTER FORTY-FIVE

MARILYN

"Marilyn, Bishop will see you now."

"Thanks, Camille!" I said to the secretary as I got up from the seat I was sitting in as I sat in the waiting area near Bishop Winston's Office on the Wednesday evening. He called and said he wanted to speak to me. So after work I was here at the church to see what it is was that he wanted to talk to me about.

"Marilyn, come in and sit down and have a seat." Bishop said as I walked into his office and sat down on the couch. He was seated at his oak wood desk.

"Now, I called you here for a couple things. First, I'd like to say that I am really glad that the Lord has healed and restored your situation with Marquise. Also I want to reassure you that I don't look at you any different since the incident with you, him, and Martice. The Devil stays busy, and we gotta keep him under our feet daily! These months have given you some time to cool off, and Marquise as well. He told me to let you know that he will be coming back home to stay until his place is done and ready in November. He's found an apartment in Palos Hills, very nice complex." I shook my head as Bishop Winston continued to talk.

"Marilyn, one of the other things that I want to talk to you about is Martice." I looked at Bishop and braced myself for what he was about to say. "Finding out that he was a homosexual was the hardest thing to grasp. I stand behind the truth and don't exchange it for any type of lie! It's just like any other sin that I preach against. Just like that Sunday when I felt the presence of that spirit in the church house, I had to preach against it, but I also have to teach that we have to be in prayer and show love. Not to pacify anything, but love is something that I most definitely preach. Love and prayer for those whose ways we don't understand, and whose ways are not our ways. I try to preach that we learn to pray that the Lord heals them with the same saving grace that we proclaim saved us."

I was hearing Bishop but I was not for accepting Martice's lifestyle! I loved Martice, but his lifestyle is wrong and I was not about to reason with it.

Bishop continued on breaking me out of my thoughts. "Marilyn, if something happens to Martice, will you be able to live with yourself?" I looked at Bishop and he met my look, he sensed that this was something I was not about to let go of. "Marilyn, I'm not asking you to give up nothing that you believe in, but you have got to search inside yourself. Let the Lord touch your heart to teach you how love and not hate! Hate the sin! Not your child!"

Bishops words shook me, but what he said next knocked me off my feet. "And just to let you know, I always knew Josiah was Marquise's real daddy. This is why I felt the need to be a little closer to him. You didn't have to tell me, the Lord revealed it to me. Marilyn, you need to find your quiet place and talk to God about any, and all, the demons that you are battling with. I will be praying for you." Bishop got up from his desk as he was making his final statement, and walked out of his office.

I was shocked, more so stunned. I could not believe that Bishop Winston knew about my affair with Josiah all this time. I grabbed my purse and keys from the table, got up, and walked toward the exit doors of the church.

CHAPTER FORTY-SIX

MARTICE

Lil Kim's "Not Tonight" song blared out of the speakers at Hydrate and I was actually enjoying myself dancing on the floor with Treyshawn.

"Bitch, you know this my song, chile!" He said laughing and twirling. I shook my head and drunk the rest of my drink. There was also a contest going on tonight, just like the one I entered back in May. I would be presenting the award this time since I was the winner of the previous contest. The song ended and Treyshawn and I headed back over to the table where we were sitting. I was wondering if Andre was going to make an entrance tonight. Things were getting kinda rocky at home, which I did not share with Treyshawn at all this past week.

First, Andre kept getting texts from Sweet Georgia Brown's, an old folks club in Country Club Hills, a south suburb in Chicago. Every time his phone lit up he would call the number and go into the bathroom. I finally got so fed up, I asked him about it and he said they were conducting business with him and his family about an upcoming birthday party for his mother. Then some of the selfie pictures that he was posting on Facebook and Instagram were getting likes and hidden message comments from different gay dudes who I knew to be very whorish. As my lurking and investigation took on a life of its own, I became so angry about it that I had to bring my concerns to him about it.

He went off and told me not to start that crazy, insecure bullshit! He would get turned off really quick by it and days would go by and we wouldn't be intimate. To make matters worse, he didn't come in from his night out on Friday night until 7 am this morning. As he slide in the room trying to not wake me, I opened my eyes and listened for his every move while my back was turned away from the bedroom door. Andre didn't even utter good morning to me, he just went straight to the shower and then came and got in the bed. It hurt because he didn't even cuddle with me like he'd do in the past; he just turned the opposite way and went to sleep. I thought about all this as I asked the bartender to give me a rum and coke.

"I hope it's some decent acts tonight, honey." Treyshawn said breaking me from my thought. "And I hope they have some acts that can match you from your last performance, at that!" Treyshawn said sipping his drink.

"I'm sure it will be." I said dryly not really into the conversation.

"I hope so, honey!" Treyshawn said turning his attention towards the door. "Chile, there go your, boo." He said as I saw Andre and his crew walk in the door and toward the VIP section. I looked and turned in his direction as the evening's show was about to start.

The announcer had said the first contestant's name. He was some Black and Brazilian looking guy who had a cut up body, just like mine, and an ass that put Kim Kardashian to shame. I heard a few cheers and some yelling, "Alright, Davian, kill it!" Ushers' "Good Kisser" boomed out of the speakers. As I watched this Davian dude, I had to admit that he had some moves. By the way he was moving he had to be a stripper. No average dancer had moves that good and, not to mention, the crowd was loving it. He popped his booty ten times better than I did at the last contest, got down and crawled on the ground, and made it clap. The crowd was egging him on. Treyshawn's mouth was on the floor. I

IT'S GONNA RAIN

scanned the crowd at the different expressions until my eyes settled on Andre, and instantly my faced turned evil and my heart filled with jealousy.

Andre damn near had his tongue hanging out of his fucking mouth. Then I looked back at the stage and I saw the Davian dude facing Andre. He was dancing intentionally for Andre and licking his lips and all other kinds of seductive shit. I saw Andre sink a little in the seat while grabbing his dick and squeezing it sneakily. Unless you were really paying attention, you would have never seen Andre doing it. The song finally ended and Davian took a bow, waved at the crowd, and then turned to Andre and gave him a wink. I was beyond pissed. Treyshawn looked at me and knew, at that point, the Sagittarian was about to come out of me. I looked at Davian and before I could say anything the next act was up.

I was so focused on what Davian and Andre were doing, I didn't even realize the last act was done and they were calling my name to announce the winner. I was pissed that this man was sitting up under my man, all cuddle up and shit like he was Andre's new main squeeze. I felt the blood rush to my head, tonight a bitch was going to try me, and a bitch was going to get that ass stomped.

"Chile, don't act a fool up in here! Check that ass when you get home!" Treyshawn said looking at me as if he knew I was about to cut up and clown.

When I heard my name being called again to announce the winner, I walked to the stage, spoke to everyone making small conversation before I opened the envelope to see who the winner of tonight's contest was.

I fumbled around with the envelope, read the name, and spoke, "And the winner of the Summer 2015 Hydrate Dance Off Bash is, " Usher's "Good Kisser" by Davian." I didn't even get the words out good before everyone rose to their feet and gave a thunderous applause for him.

"I smiled, handed him the award, and came in to give him a hug. Just as I embraced him I whispered in his ear, "Bitch, don't get tossed up in here tonight, you sittin' up under my man." I drew back from the hug and so did he. Davian looked at me with a look of horror on his face but a half smile. I looked at him with the Devil's grin and continued to clap and then turned my attention to Andre, who knew I had said something out of whack. His facial expression was priceless, but mine took the mutha-fuckin cake.

CHAPTER FORTY-SEVEN

MARQUISE

I loved the temporary place that Bishop provided for me during my time away from my mother's house, but I had to admit that there was no place like your own home - or in my case my soon to be old home. I was happy to have finally put all my bags away and was ready to eat the nice home cooked meal my mother had prepared. She even told me to invite Isis over, which I happily did. They talked about the colors for the wedding and the guests that were invited. We talked like old times, laughed like old times, and I was glad to be back at home, even though it was going to be a short time for me. After I returned home from taking Isis home, I sat on the couch and had a talk with my mother.

258

"Ma, how you feeling?" I asked her sitting on the opposite couch.

"Feeling good, baby, just some things on my mind but it's nothin' that God will not take care of." She said turning on the television, there was an old live broadcast recording of Dr. Charles G. Hayes & Cosmopolitan Church of Prayers Choir singing "He Shall Feed His Flock" on the television. They were really killing the song and my mother closed her eyes and rocked back and forth to the music and words. The altos and sopranos started singing, "through the storm and the rain, through sickness and pain, I will not complain."

I saw my mother raise her hands, she was feeling the song. She opened her eyes as the altos and sopranos sung their part once more. My mother grabbed some tissue and started dabbing at her eyes as one of the sopranos hit a high note. I closed my eyes and said a silent prayer, then I opened them and my mother spoke.

"I have always been strong. I was taught to be strong in any situation. I just don't know why I can't be strong at this point in my life." She said.

"Ma, you are strong, the Devil wants you to keep thinking about your past and the mistakes you've made. Loose it and let it go!" I said trying to encourage her. "You are healed and set free. You have taught me all I know about the Lord, and his power, and for that, ma, I love and thank you! For when I was out on the streets selling weed and dope, you still prayed for me and I got it together quickly! I Love you, ma. Thank you for preparing me to be a good man for Isis. I'm even thankful to dad, even though he was not my real dad, and even though he made some mistakes, for taking me in as his own, and on positive notes showing me how to be a man." I said as my mother shook her head slowly at me.

"I guess my fear was always about not wanting to let go. Out of you and Martice, I have always held you at a high standard because of who your real daddy was, I loved him. But in God's eyes it was wrong. But you are a grown man, Marquise Johnson, and I am taking the hold that I have on you off. You're going to marry that beautiful girl and I believe you're going to make her happy. She is lucky to have found someone like you, I am honored to have raised you, and you were a blessing from God despite of the situation." She said smiling at me.

I hugged my mother, kissed her on the forehead, and told her good night. I left her sitting on the couch, where she eventually closed her eyes, and feel asleep herself.

CHAPTER FORTY-EIGHT

MARILYN

Reminiscing back to 1993: I screamed at the top of my lungs and cried out in pain moving my head from side to side.

"Baby, push! I see the head and he got a head full of hair!" Rick said laughing.

"Come on, Marilyn, give me another one!" Dr. Roberts said.

I bore down as hard as I could grabbing onto Rick's hands squeezing as hard as I could. I had been at this for thirty-six hours and I was ready for it to end.

"We just need one more push, he's almost out!" Dr. Roberts said. It felt like I was being ripped open, I gave it one more as the tears came down my face.

"LORDDDDDDDDD JESUSSSS!!! AHHHHHHHHH!!!!" I yelled as everyone shouted praises and I heard a baby crying.

"Baby, he is so beautiful!" Rick said as he was holding Martice. I wanted to see him, to see what I had went through for thirty-six hours of labor for. I don't remember Marquise even being that much trouble, but this second go 'round, I thought I was going to die in this hospital bed. I'm so glad I'd made up in my mind that I wasn't having any more children after Martice. Rick handed to me wrapped up baby. It was such a precious moment as he stared at me and I looked at him. "Hello, Martice Rick Johnson." I said as I kissed him on the cheek. He yawned and continued to blink and stare at me. My heart soften, I kissed Rick, and turned my attention back to the baby. I smiled as he had closed his little eyelids; he was tired and so was I.

CHAPTER FORTY-NINE

MARTICE

Andre called himself pissed and didn't come home after the club that night after the incident with Davian. I acted like I didn't care but I did. I called him and called him to no avail; eventually it started to go right to voicemail after one ring.

"You're gonna answer this damn phone!" I yelled out to the air as I kept dialing and dialing his number. And once again, after one ring, it kept going straight to voicemail. I called Treyshawn's phone and he answered after two rings.

"Chile, wassup!" He could hear me breathing strangely, "What's the matter?" He asked concerned.

"Andre ass not answering the damn phone! I bet he with that muthafuckin bitch from the club!" I said yelling.

"Martice, chile, calm down, damn!" Treyshawn said.

I started pacing back and forth. I was on fire with anger. "Hold on!" I told Treyshawn. I dialed the number and, again, it just rung and rung and rung. I hung it up and kept calling him.

"Chile, stop callin' him!" Treyshawn yelled.

"Dial this number for me!" I said to him so he could shut the hell up.

"No, honey, I'm not getting involved in y'all shit." Treyshawn said.

"Treyshawn, please, just dial the number!" I said frantically.

I heard him smack his lips, then after a five second pause, he said, "Give me the number!" I gave him the number, he clicked over, and came back in when the other line started ringing.

"Hello?" Andre's voice said very low after three rings.

"WHERE YOU AT?!?!" I yelled.

"WHY?!" He snapped back.

"What you mean, why? Why are you playing fuckin' games with me right now, Andre?!" I said getting upset cause I could tell he had a crowd around him and he was showing out for them.

"Yo, I'll talk to you later I don't have time for this shit, you trippin' out and sounding real coo, coo right now." He said laughing and so did whoever he was around in the background.

"So you got a little crowd and you gonna show your ass. For real, Andre?!" I yelled as I was jumping up off the couch.

"Like I said, I gotta go. I'm not about to be holdin' this phone arguin' wit yo ass. You trippin' the fuck out, man, for real." He yelled.

"When you comin' home?" I asked.

"When I feel like it. Damn!" He said.

I was getting heated very quickly, he was drunk and showing out for whomever he was hanging out with.

"When you feel like it?" What the fuck? I don't appreciate you tryin' to front cause you got a crowd of people around you too." I said trying to get him to see it my way.

"Man, I gotta go I'm not about to be on this phone and keep arguing with your ass." He said.

"Don't have your ass here within an hour!" I said through clenched teeth. I wasn't for this shit tonight, and I definitely was about to go back and forth. He wanted to show out like an ass because he had a crowd. I would let them know that he had, indeed, had me in the background acting like fool.

"What you gonna do if I don't come to the crib?" He asked carelessly and then started laughing.

"Don't act like I can't find you." I said.

"Well, let's just see if you can!" He said and then the line went click.

"Oop!" Treyshawn said.

"I know his ass did not just hang the phone up??" I said.

"Hold on." Treyshawn said clicking over and dialing the number again, but this time it rang once for him and went straight to voicemail.

"Chileeeee, this too many things tonight!" Treyshawn said.

I sat down on the couch and looked at the wall; I couldn't believe this shit was happening. I didn't understand why Andre was acting the way that he was.

"Martice, what you gonna do, honey?" Treyshawn asked me. I just got quiet and didn't say anything. "You need to leave his ass alone, fuck him! You been putting up with his shit for a minute now, but I told you what to expect, honey. Andre just like the rest of them." Treyshawn added.

I really did not feel like talking about it. And I just wanted to lay down and go to sleep. "Chile, I'll call you tomorrow." I said.

"Goodnite." Treyshawn said and I hit the end button on the phone.

The next morning I woke up and realized I was still laying on the couch. I squinted my eyes and looked at the time on my phone, 9:15 am it said. I sat up and heard Andre in the bedroom. He was going through the closet and drawers. I noticed garbage bags were laid on the bed. *Was he cleaning his stuff out? And why?* I thought to myself. He noticed I was woke, looked at me for a second, then continued to do what he was doing.

"You gonna act like last night didn't happen?" I said.

He looked at me again and then went into the bathroom. I stared at him like he had lost his damn mind.

"I asked you a question!" I said.

"But that don't mean I have to give you an answer." He replied back.

"And I'm just supposed to be okay with that? You out late not telling me nothing nowadays, flirtin' in my face with other sissies at the club, and talking to me any kinda way. I can't deal with this, Andre!" I yelled at him.

"Well if you can't, you can get your shit and go, as a matter of fact. That's why I took these bags out for you, so you can start getting your shit together. Fuck what I said about next week, you can go stay with Treyshawn for good. Or how about taking your ass back home to your holy rollin' mama!" He spat out evilly at me.

My mouth dropped and my heart sank. I could not believe he was putting me out. The only thing I was hearing right now was my mother's voice in my head, "He ain't gonna do nothin', but get tired of your ass and put you out!" And, boy, she never lied about that.

This was what I didn't want to be bothered with, to deal with, to subject myself to, the selfishness of a gay male I called myself being in a relationship with. This was the only concern in this lifestyle - the "me" mentality of most of the gays. Me! Me! Me! Me! All about me and the selfishness, and the I don't give a fuck about your feelings attitude that the men of this lifestyle carried.

"You know damn well I can't go back to my mother's house. Because of you is why I was put out in the first place. And then you're going to turn around, just like that, and put

268

me out, too?" I said looking at him getting angry and hurt at the same damn time.

"HELL YEAH! Get your shit and get out! This shit not working anymore. I don't have to explain nothing to you, so don't sit and look at me like I owe you an explanation, get the shit that you have, and get out my crib!" He said walking past me and shaking his head mumbling under his breathe.

"Well give me my fucking money back!" I said walking up on him.

"Martice, don't walk up on me like you crazy!"

"Well give me the money that I gave you!" I yelled still in his face. I wasn't backing down for shit, and he was going to give me that money I gave him back.

"You will get it when I give that little petty ass money back to your ass!" He said with the most arrogance.

"Well, go get my petty ass little money, then!" I yelled. "If you don't have my money I ain't going nowhere until you give it to me." I smiled and sat down on the couch. He could just try putting me out, but I wasn't going anywhere until he gave me back that money.

Andre raised his eyebrows, looked back at me, smiled, and said, "You can leave like someone who has some sense, or I can have the cops come and put your ass out. Which would you like it to be?"

CHAPTER FIFTY

MARQUISE

I was on cloud nine. The Lord definitely was in the blessing business. I had just received the call that I had been waiting for. Betzler Enterprises, located in downtown Chicago had offered me a full-time position as their IT technician making seventy grand a year. I called and told my mother and Isis, who both were just as excited for me.

My brother crossed my mind, I dialed his number, but got no answer. I left him a voicemail message to call me as soon as he got the message. I was ready to celebrate and wanting my family and Isis to be there to do so. I heard my phone ring and it was Martice calling me back.

"Hey, bro, you called?" He asked.

"Yeah, man. I just got offered a full-time gig at Betzler downtown making seventy thousand a year!" I practically yelled into the phone.

"Congrats, bro! That's good!" He said but I could tell in his voice something was not right.

"Bro, you okay?" I asked him. There was a long pause before he responded.

"Yea, I'm good. How are you and ma?" He asked.

"Well I'm good, but why don't you come by and see her and find out for yourself." I said to him then there was another long pause. "Martice? You still here, bro?" I asked him.

"Yeah, but listen, I got some things to take care of. Can I call you back a little later?" He asked me.

"Yea, no problem, and don't forget what I just told you, bro." I said to him.

"Gotcha!" He said and hung up the line.

CHAPTER FIFTY-ONE

MARILYN

I fanned myself from the choir stand, as I listened to Bishop Winston speak about the trials and tribulations of this life and how we have to persevere while down here on earth. I saw Marquise smile and yell out his usual Baptist "wells" each time Bishop Winston spoke on an important topic.

"Powerhouse, God did not say things were goin' to be a garden of flowers while we're livin' on this earth! He said we was gonna go through some things down here! But the trouble don't last always!"

"Say that, Bishop!" I yelled in my soprano voice and continued to fan myself a little. I didn't know if they needed to cut the air up a little more but it was definitely hot in the sanctuary this morning during service.

"I thank the Lord that he is the God of another chance. He is not like man who will let you down! Seek ye first the kingdom of God…" Bishop Winston couldn't even get it out all the way before someone one was up on their feet shouting. "I say the Lord will provide! He will give you any and everything you need when you wait on him! Wait on him and keep the faith that he will do whatever you ask of him!" Bishop yelled into mic.

"Daily I shalllllll worship theeeee… Lamb of God who died for meeee!!" Bishop sung into the mic as me and the entire choir stood on our feet behind him, with Marquise and the other associate minsters doing the same.

The entire church was singing along with Bishop as he yelled, "Sing it from your heart!" Welcoming in the Holy Ghost as the screams and cries rang out. I rocked from side to side and waved my hand in the air as Bishop continued to sing his favorite song, which always tore the church up.

"And I know the Lord!!!! Will make a wayyyyyyy, yes he will!" Bishop switched up to sing and the choir came behind him with "Ooooooohhhhhh, yesss he willlll!"

The bass guitar started to play and the organ chimed in giving it that churchy, blues feel, that's when all the seasoned saints in the congregation stood on their feet, waving their hands and singing along. Sister Velma Springs jumped up, pointed at Bishop, and yelled, "Go 'head! That's it right there!"

"He'll makeeeeeeeeeeeeeee a wayyyyyyyyyyyyyyyyy for you! He will surely, surely, surely bring you through. I know the Lordddddddd!" Bishop hollered and the choir came in with "I know the Lordddd, will make a wayyyyyyyy, ooooooh, yesss he will!!!!" Bishop went into his course and the choir backed him with "Yes, he will; yes, he will; yes, he will!"

I knew at that point it was going to be one of those services. I laid the fan down and started feeling the song myself. The Lord was in Powerhouse this morning. Saints that I normally didn't see lift a finger were up on their feet singing along. Once the special came the entire church was tore up. The choir kept repeating, "He did it, he made a way."

Sister Velma started shouting and screaming and a lady next to her on the same row started fanning her, trying to calm her down as the ushers rushed to help out. Once one person started, it was a domino effect. Screaming and shouting, as we continued to sing, "He did it, he made a way."

The band was definitely driving that blues feel. Bishop hollered into the mic singing his part and the church continued to go up in praise. He gave Solomon the signal and he ended the song with us yelling out one more time, "He did it! He made a way!"

The congregation clapped and the praise for God resonated all over the sanctuary. Sam, our other director, whispered something to the organist, and I heard the lyrics to a famous melody he played out.

"Sing it! Sing it!" Bishop yelled at the choir as we laughed while he took his seat.

"If you confess the Lord!!!! Call him up!" The break in the music played as we continued singing. "If you confess the Lorddddddddddd, call him up!!!" We sang and clapped. Solomon was into it as we jumped from one song in the medley to the next with the congregation staying on their feet, clapping and yelling for us to "go 'head and sing!"

"Are you ready! Are you ready! Yes I'm ready! Forrr the coming of the Lord! Are you ready! Are you ready! Yes I'm ready! Forr the coming of the Lord! Be ye also ready! Be ye also ready!" Once we got to that one, it was like a party was taking place. I moved my head from side to side, clapping my hands, and really feeling the soprano part of that song as my voice rang out!

On to the next song we sanged. "Do not! Pass me by! Do not! Pass me by!" I screamed in my soprano voice as the altos and tenors joined in on their parts. Solomon flipped, turned, and matrixed his arms directing us. He stopped, looked at the organ player, the picture of his mother was sitting on the top of it, he grabbed it, paused, and sat down on the steps, hugging it as tears streamed down his face.

Sam ran over and started directing us, which really sent the church in shock. Sam had not directed in years and he still had in him what he passed off to Solomon. It was amazing to see him, as he jigged, and moved his hands and arms in directing us. Some of the congregants looked on, wondering what was happening, but others and myself knew. As one of the ushers in the pulpit kneeled, and rubbed Solomon's back. He missed Mabel, His mother. But for some reason I could feel her spirit in the service today.

"Whatever! The Problem! I put it all in his hands! Whatever the Problem! I put it all in his hands!" We sung out, and all of a sudden, out of nowhere, I felt something and my emotions flowed out. I dropped down in my seat, and the entire soprano section consoled me. I felt Marquise come over, and sit next to me. As I laid my head on his shoulder, and I cried. He rubbed my shoulder with his hand, but I could not stop crying as I felt the shadows of people standing over me, I heard Bishop Winston's voice praying over me with his hand on my other shoulder. It was at that very moment, I knew, I missed Martice.

CHAPTER FIFTY-TWO

MARTICE

I sat at Treyshawn's house with him at his kitchen table eating. It had been a week since I had seen or spoken to Andre, and he still had not given me back that damn money. He was not answering my phone calls or texts.

"Chile, you might as well hang that up and kiss that money goodbye!" Treyshawn said.

"I jumped up and ran to the bathroom. I started scratching the inside of my ass and it burned a little. I hesitated, sat down on the toilet, then I tried to take a shit and blood came out with the stool. I immediately froze up." I wiped my ass, flushed the toilet, washed my hands, and came back out to the kitchen table. I sat back down with Treyshawn looking crazy.

"Chile, you okay?" Treyshawn asked as he saw the look on my face.

"I was bleeding from the ass!" I said dazed and amazed.

"WHAT!?" Treyshawn said jumping up from the table in his most dramatic self.

"Yes, I'm bleeding from the ass!" I repeated it.

"Chile, have you been tested since you started dating Andre?" I got quiet and turned my face to the window. "MARTICE?! BITCH, WHAT THE FUCK IS WRONG WITH YOU!?!?!" He yelled at me.

"Nothin'!" I yelled back and started crying uncontrollably.

"Chile, it's time for me to do mine, and what a perfect day than today to go down to Aunt Martha's! Go get dressed!" He said getting up and going to his room.

I sat at the table drying my eyes. Never in a million years would I have thought that I needed to go and have an STD test. I've played it safe and used condoms. Andre and I started out using condoms, but I allowed it to stop when I knew we were in a relationship and it got serious. I said a prayer to God, got up, and headed to the spare room

Treyshawn had me staying in to get my clothes together to shower and go to the clinic with him.

CHAPTER FIFTY-THREE

MARQUISE

The first week of training at Betzler was dynamic. I was doing something that I loved, and it was paying me well. I even gave my mother an extra two thousand dollars out of one of my checks just for her to have stashed away for a rainy day. She thanked me, but also told me I didn't have to do it. My response was that I wanted to.

She was getting ready to go on vacation in two weeks to L.A. to see my grandmother. I wished I could go, I loved the Baldwin Hills area, but seeing I just started my new job I knew I had to put all vacations on hold for a while. It just seemed so surreal with everything happening for me and so fast.

Because I loved to sing I decided that I would pick up side gigs to sing for events. This weekend I had picked up a gig to sing for a wedding. I love it when people would be so amazed by my voice – it was definitely a gift from God. My mother said it also came from my father – I didn't know he could sing as well. My mother asked me if I wanted to see an old converted to DVD video of him preaching at Powerhouse for one of Bishop Winston's pastor's anniversary. I did, and I was quiet the entire time. This man was the older, original version of me. Everything about him, I was. His mannerisms, the way he preached, and the way he sang. If I didn't know this was my father before now, I would have definitely known after watching this video. He had me in awe of him. He even had the same smile as me; I was really this dude's son.

I almost felt a little sad the way that his life had to end, but I wondered if the Lord had spared him and let him enter into the gates of heaven. I cut the TV off and started singing the song that he ended his sermon with going to my room to call it a night, my mother had long left me to watch alone.

CHAPTER FIFTY-FOUR

MARILYN

"Mama, I cannot wait to get to L.A. to relax!" I said to her while we were on the phone as I was sitting at my desk. It was the following Monday and I was already in vacation mode, not thinking about anything but rest and relaxation.

"Well, just don't get here getting on my damn nerves!" She said and I laughed. "Still have not heard from Martice?" She asked me.

"Nope." I said thinking about him a little.

"Marilyn, have you called him?" She asked me sternly.

"Yes, mama! He won't return my phone calls." I said getting up and getting a bottle of apple juice out of the mini refrigerator I had in my office.

"Well you made the first move, so now you just have to let it play itself out." Mama's voice quickly changed tones. "Listen, I may have someone here you might be interested in. He's your age, single, has a daughter who is grown like Marquise and Martice. He just moved on the block. He's a marketing exec., tall, dark-skinned, goes to the gym every other day and runs around the neighborhood. He just turned forty-six, Colgate smile, drives an Audi, and I already told him about you." She said with excitement in her voice.

"And why did you do that, mama?" I asked.

"Because, Marilyn, you need a man, honey!" She said and fell out laughing.

"Mama, I do just fine, okay." I responded getting irritated.

"No you don't. You act like some old dried up ass hag. Nit picking and all. It's time for you to get some excitement in your life. Time for you to get Marilyn back!"

I looked at the phone like I had heard enough. I could not believe my mother had a date already set up and waiting for me when I got to L.A. "Mama, how you know I didn't have someone coming with me?" I asked her.

"Cause I know you don't. Anyway, you better had let me know that in the first place. You know I don't take kind to just anybody, especially a man, coming up in my house and I don't know about him." She said and I laughed. "Yeah, you better laugh that shit up. You and him would have been on the first thing smoking back to Chicago after I get done cussing you out and laying into him." She said.

"Mama, you something else."

"No, honey, I'm Ethelyn Jenkins! That's who I am!" She said and started laughing with me.

"Mama, I just want to say we have not always seen eye to eye on everything, but I am thankful for forgiveness and the fact that this whole mess has passed over. I just want to say that I love you." I said to her trying not to cry. It's something I have been doing a lot of lately.

"And even though you and Marian get on my nerves, I would have not wanted no other daughters than you two. So, baby, I love you, too!" She said.

We laughed and then I added Marian to our call via three-way, and we had another fifteen minute conversation before we all parted ways for the day.

JEFFERY ROSHELL

CHAPTER FIFTY-FIVE

MARTICE

I was tested for everything under the sun at the clinic and they told me I should hear from them within a week or so. I was nervous and could not stop thinking about it. Treyshawn told me to relax but that was virtually impossible with the weight of what was going on looming in my mind. I still had not heard from Andre, and every time I went by his apartment, or called his house phone, no one was there.

As I was preoccupied with trying to get in touch with Andre, Tuesday of the following week I received a call from a number that I did not recognize.

With hesitation, I answered the phone. "Hello?"

"Hello, I was looking for Martice Johnson?" The voice said.

"Yes, this is me." I responded.

"Hello, Martice! This is Aunt Martha's giving you a call." As the voice was speaking, I frantically waved at Treyshawn mouthing to him that Aunt Martha's was on the phone. The voice continued, "You came in for testing on last Thursday, we need you to come in and see the doctor as soon as you can regarding your test results."

"Okay." I said nervously and hung up the phone. I immediately looked at Treyshawn who was curiously looking on.

"Chile, what they say?" Treyshawn ask and then his phones started lighting up and vibrating. "Wait! Hold on my phone is ringing now..." Treyshawn said and then answering it. I watched on as he spoke to the mysterious caller. "Okay. Okay, thank you. Um-hum, goodbye." He said as he hung up the phone. He smiled and then said, "Chile, a clean bill of health, honey. They told me there's nothing wrong! All test came back negative!"

I looked at Treyshawn, smiled a little but sat down on the couch across from him. He looked at me and his expression changed.

"They told me I needed to come in as soon as possible." I said swallowing the lump in my throat.

"Now, chile, just calm down, okay. You don't know what's going on, yet, until you go in there. Whatever it is I am here for you. Do you wanna go now?" He asked.

"Yes!" I said without hesitation as we both got up and got in his car heading over to the clinic.

I signed in once I got to the reception area and waited to be called. One of the nurses came and got me and I followed her into a room. She told me that the doctor was next door with another patient and she would be in with me shortly. My life started flashing before my eyes from a child to youth, up until now. I thought about the good and the bad times that I had endured, the things that life's lessons had taught me. I closed my eyes, but opened them immediately when I heard a loud, shrill scream coming from the next room. It came from the soul I had never heard that before.

"NOOOOOOO!! OH MY, GOODDD!! NOOOO! NOOOO! NOOOO!" Was all the voice kept screaming. I jumped up, ran out of the room, and out the door with Treyshawn on my heels. I could faintly hear the nurse yelling for me to come back.

We got back to Treyshawn's house after a quiet ride from the clinic.

"Why did you get up and leave?" He asked me.

I wasn't listening to him. I went to the room I stayed in and grabbed the box that was delivered for Andre last week and went to the kitchen.

"These boxes have come for him every month. This last one, I took it because I want to know what's in it." I said to Treyshawn who made a crazy face looking at me.

"Well, chile, open it!" He said as I sat down across from him and I did just that. Once I opened it the box was full of pill bottles. I pulled one of the bottles out and read the label and studied the words. "Gen-vo-ya…" I began to sound out and then Treyshawn cut me off.

"BITCH! WHAT DID YOU JUST SAY???" Treyshawn asked me with a shocked look on his face.

"It says, 'Genvoya' on this bottle. What the hell is Genvoya?" I read down the bottle description and dropped it immediately damn near falling out of the chair. Treyshawn got up and grabbed me, rocking me back and forth in his arms as I screamed and cried in horror with tears flowing down my face.

CHAPTER FIFTY-SIX

MARQUISE

It was very warm for a Friday night; I had taken Isis to the movies to see the new Kevin hart movie. What was crazy was the sky was like a blackish pink and there was no reporting of a tornado or severe thunderstorm warning. I called my mother and told her that I would be home soon; it was working on 11 pm. Mama and I both had to be at the church for an early Saturday morning meeting. I kissed Isis goodnight dropping her off and made it home within fifteen minutes. I got out of my car, still looking towards the sky. The sky was so strange that night, it just seemed like something was going to happen, the atmosphere did not feel right at all. I walked up the steps, cut the alarm off and then back on once I got into the house. Took a shower and passed off to sleep.

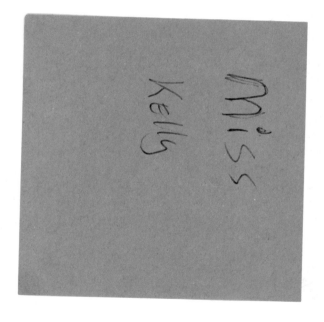

CHAPTER FIFTY-SEVEN

MARILYN

I had Inspiration 1288 AM radio playing while I slept every night. I love having it on at night because they would play the old, slow, Gospel songs that would soothe you and put you to sleep. Rev. James Cleveland's "Peace Be Still" was playing and it woke me up when I heard him sing the part, "The wind and the rain shall obey thy will." I looked around in my dark room and felt that something was not right. Then all of a sudden my cell phone lit up and across the screen read Martice's name, I answered it immediately.

"Hello?" I said.

"Ma, help me, please!! Please pray for me, please!!" Martice said crying furiously.

"Martice, calm down what's wrong?" I asked him with a crazy look on my face from just waking up.

"I never meant to do what I did to you, I'm sorry!" He said sobbing. I could tell that he wasn't himself.

"Martice?? What is going on?" I asked him sternly.

"You were right, and now I'm going to die! But I'm going to kill him first! I can't deal with this! I can't deal with being sick for the rest of my life! He killed me, ma! He killed me! I should have listened to you!" He said with so much agony in his voice.

I sat all the way up in the bed, now I was fully awake, trying to listen to what Martice was saying - trying to make some sense of it. As I'm listening to Martice, Rev. Cleveland and The Choir sounded as if they were getting louder and louder. "As the ship was being tossed at sea!" The song sanged out in the most melodramatic way.

"Martice, who is tryin' to kill you? What's goin on, baby? Talk to me!" I screamed, but the phone went dead.

I had never rushed so fast in my life to get clothes on take a scarf off my head and put shoes on my feet. I called out to Marquise and he flew down the steps asking me what was wrong? I told him to put on his shoes now and to take me where Martice was in Englewood.

CHAPTER FIFTY-EIGHT

MARTICE

I stared straight ahead as Treyshawn drove to Andre's apartment. "Now, chile, you said you was just goin' over here to let him know that you know and that's it. Don't be no fool and do nothing with that gun!" He said looking at me and the gun.

I just stared straight ahead quietly awaiting to get to our destination. At this moment I hear nothing or nobody, I had one agenda only. We pulled up to the apartment complex, it was 2 am. I saw his Charger outside so I knew he was definitely home.

"So, bitch, you gonna knock on the door? How we gonna do this?" Treyshawn asked as we walked around the back and up the stairs to the last floor. We stood in front of the door. "Bitch, bang on it like the police!" Treyshawn said.

I looked at him, put the gun in my pocket, and took out a spare key I had made at Walmart a few weeks ago. I put it in the lock and turned it.

Treyshawn dropped his mouth and whispered, "Bitchhhhhh, you ain't joke!"

I nodded to him and we tip-toed into the apartment. I halfway closed the door and tip-toed around the living room to the bedroom. I could see his silhouette and someone else's laying down, hugged up in the bed with him. It was Davian from the club. Treyshawn looked at me and I looked at him and began to turn red. We both got closer inside the bedroom and Andre's eyelids started flittering, and as if he had saw a ghost. He jumped up quickly, pushing Davian off him.

"HOW THE FUCK YOU GET IN MY CRIB!" He yelled. I stared at him for a long time. "MARTICE, YOU AND YOUR BOY BETTA GET THE FUCK OUT OF MY CRIB BEFORE I CALL THE POLICE! CRAZY ASS GOT EXTRA KEYS TO MY SHIT MADE! WHAT THE FUCK!" Andre spat out at me tryin' to cover his muscular naked body so I could not see.

Davian did the same searching for his underwear. I first pulled the pill bottle out from my pocket and threw it at him.

"Genvoya, huh? So you cannot deal with HIV alone, huh? Everybody else that you come in contact with you gotta catch it, too, huh?!" I yelled at him as he dropped his mouth. His lack of response irritated me. "I asked you a question!" I yelled as I was pulling out the gun from my other pocket. Everybody screamed as I cocked the trigger.

"So, now, you gonna kill me, huh? Well do it! I ain't got shit to live for no damn way! That's right! You and the rest of the hoes that want me will get the gift that keeps on giving. Bet you still looking for that money ain't you? I spent it! That's why I never gave it back, you just as stupid as your holy ass mama!" He said laughing"

"FUCK YOU!" I yelled and the gun went off. Pop! Pop! I heard my mother yell my name, she came running in the room she looked in horror at me and everyone else, so did my brother. Treyshawn and Davian were kneeling in the corner. I dropped the gun, turned and looked at my mother, and dropped down to my knees on the floor. I closed my eyes and just wanted to speak to God and hear from him. That was the only person that mattered to me at this particular moment.

TEN MONTHS LATER....

CHAPTER FIFTY-NINE

Marilyn

It was July of 2016. The year from the horror of summer 2015 flew by. I had just come from Sunday service, and I was getting ready to sit down and have dinner with my family. I reflected on how much a year had changed things for my family. Marquise and Isis were married and expecting a baby boy in December of 2016. And Martice had made a career change and had become an STD Counselor with a local clinic.

After the incident with Andre, he decided he wanted to help others by sharing his testimony with those who were not as fortunate as him. He knew that he could also help those who could look at his story and lead them into not making the same careless mistake with a partner – because it wasn't guaranteed that they would be as lucky as Martice was. You may be wondering what I'm talking about when I mention luck.

Well after Martice's encounter with Andre I was able to talk him into grabbing the gun off the ground and leaving immediately with Marquise and I before the police showed up. We were all grateful that Martice didn't shoot Andre and that no one got hurt that night. Martice said that when he fired those two shots above Andre's head, he was only doing it to scare him.

Although he didn't want to face the truth, I encouraged him that the main concern was to see what the results were. Marquise, me, and even Treyshawn convinced him to go back to the clinic. Turns out he tested negative for everything except for Chlamydia. He had the doctor repeat all the STD tests, especially the HIV, which again turned up with the same results. We all cried tears of joy in the doctor's office that day because we know that it was only the grace of God – for it could have been worse.

The doctor instructed Martice to come back and test again in six months, which he did. Praise God all of the tests results came back negative. It was at that moment that he

301

said he wanted to be a mentor for other young gay males to make them aware of the prevention of STDs, especially HIV.

Now, though I still stick by what I believe, I have embraced Martice for who he is and whatever lifestyle he chooses for himself. I realized this is my son, and no matter what he does, I could never hate him. I pray for him and let God lead the way and show the direction. I'm finally walking in that love that Bishop Winston told me about that day in his office. I believe it's because of my new way of thinking that Martice and I's relationship has improved drastically. Martice moved back in the house with me for right now, soon he would be ready to find his own place, but I must admit I'm enjoying his presence there.

I have been preparing myself to go to back to L.A. The marketing executive, Winston, the gentleman that lives next door to my mother, and I have been seeing each other for the past five months. I even mentioned to him that if things get a little more serious somebody is going to have to move. He asked me what I thought about palm trees and earthquakes? I turned around and asked him what was his take on good food and gunshots?

JEFFERY ROSHELL

<u>ABOUT THE AUTHOR</u>

Jeffery Roshell Is the author of the novel "Thornhill High School" he lives in Chicago Illinois, and is at work on his next novel.

Connect with Jeffery Roshell

jefferyroshell@facebook.com

www.jefferyroshell.net

IG: authorjefferyroshell

53951409R00173

Made in the USA
Columbia, SC
26 March 2019